THE WIZARD OF VENUS

The Wizard of Venus

Edgar Rice Burroughs

NEW ENGLISH LIBRARY
TIMES MIRROR

First published in the United States of America by Ace Books
in association with Edgar Rice Burroughs, Inc.

*

FIRST NEL PAPERBACK EDITION JANUARY 1973

*

NEL Books are published by
New English Library Limited from Barnard's Inn, Holborn, London, E.C.1.
Made and printed in Great Britain by Hunt Barnard Printing Ltd., Aylesbury, Bucks.

450013537

FOREWORD

I often recall my introduction to Carson Napier. 'If a female figure in a white shroud enters your bedchamber at midnight on the thirteenth day of this month, answer this letter; otherwise, do not.' That was the beginning of his letter to me – the letter that was almost consigned to a waste-basket.

Three days later, on the thirteenth, a female figure in a white shroud did enter my bedchamber at midnight. It was thus that Carson Napier convinced himself that he and I were in psychological accord and that I was the man through which his interplanetary wanderings might be transmitted.

After we had met in person, he explained to me how he had acquired this mystical power by means of which he could project whatever visions he wished to whatever distance and cause another to see them. It is by this thing that he learned from the old East Indian, Chand Kabi, that he has been able to transmit to me not only the story of his adventures upon Venus but permit me to witness many of them as truly as though I were present at his side upon The Shepherd Star.

I have often wondered why he uses this power so infrequently to meet the emergencies which so often confront him. In this, the latest story of his adventures that I have received, he has.

Honolulu
October 7, 1941

Edgar Rice Burroughs

ONE

I BELIEVE THAT IT WAS Roy Chapman Andrews who said that adventures were the result of incompetence and inefficiency, or words to that effect. If that be so, I must be the prize incompetent of two worlds; for I am always encountering the most amazing adventures.

It seems to me that I always plan intelligently, sometimes over meticulously; and then up jumps the Devil and everything goes haywire. However, in all fairness, I must admit that it is usually my fault and attributable to a definite temerariousness which is characteristic of me. I am rash. I take chances. I know that that is stupid. The thing that reflects most discredit upon my intelligence is the fact that oftentimes I know the thing I am about to do is stupid, and yet I go ahead and do it, I gamble with Death; my life is the stake. But I have a grand time, and so far I have always beaten Death to the draw.

The misadventure which altered the direction of flight of my rocket ship, so that I landed on Venus instead of Mars, was the result of a minor miscalculation by one of America's most famous astronomers whose figures were checked and rechecked by several of his equally erudite fellows, as well as by myself. I feel that there was no lack of intelligence, no stupidity here; yet the result was a sequence of adventures such as probably never have befallen any other man.

I shall leave it to whoever may chance to read of this, my latest adventure, as to how much of chance and how much of stupidity were responsible for it. You are the judge. Arrange your reading lamp a little to the left of and just behind your favorite chair, and scan the evidence.

I knew Ero Shan in Havatoo, that model city beside the River of Death. He was my best friend there. He helped me build the first aeroplane to fly the empty skies of Venus. Duare called it an anotar, or bird-ship; and in it she and I escaped from Havatoo after the miscarriage of justice which had condemned her to death.

The next time I saw Ero Shan he was hanging on a wall in the museum of natural history in the city of Voo-ad, paralyzed from the neck down. Duare and I were hanging beside him in the same condition. He told me that he, with the assistance of some of the best scientific minds in Havatoo, had succeeded in building another anotar and that during a trial flight he had encountered the same terrific storm that had blown Duare and me thousands of miles off our course, with the result that he had been compelled to make a forced landing near Voo-ad, where he had ended up as an exhibit for hundreds of amoeba people to gawp at daily.

When we escaped, we took Ero Shan with us; and after a series of harrowing adventures we reached Sanara, the capital of Korva, which is a country on the continent of Anlap. Korva is the only country on Venus that Duare and I can call our own. I had fought for it against the blood-mad Zanies. I had saved the life of the little daughter of the present jong, or emperor, my good friend Taman; and because of these things he had adopted me as his son.

I am, therefore, Tanjong of Korva; and when Duare and I returned to Sanara after more than a year's absence, we received, both figuratively and literally, a royal welcome; for they had long since given up all hope of ever seeing us again.

We were banquetted and feted for days; and, that the people might see us and welcome us home, we toured the city in a royal howdah on the back of a gorgeously trapped gantor, one of those leviathan beasts of burden whose size might dwarf the mammoth or the mastodon. Two hundred of these great beasts, bearing nobles and warriors, formed our cortege. At sight of us the people seemed to go mad with joy, attesting our popularity and the beauty of Duare.

At last we had a home, and we were home. We looked forward to long years of peace and happiness. No more travel, no more adventures for us! We were through. I didn't know whether crown princes like to wear carpet slippers and sit with their feet on a desk and smoke a pipe and read of an evening, but that is what I wanted to do. You shall see how I did it.

TWO

I HAD PROMISED ERO SHAN that I would design and help him build an anotar in which he could fly back to Havatoo; and as Taman wished me to supervise the building of some for the Korvan army, we had two under construction at the same time.

While this work was in progress I designed and had fabricated an entirely new type of parachute which opened instantaneously and descended very slowly. It could also be guided by flaps which opened and closed holes in the fabric. Tests eventually demonstrated that it could be used safely at an altitude of only two hundred feet.

I might note here, parenthetically, that I was working on an even more efficient safety device at the time that Fate decreed new and unwelcome adventures for me; thus terminating my experiments. The fuel used in the silent motor of my anotar I have described several times before in recounting former adventures. It consists of a substance known as *lor*, which contains an element called *yor-san* and another element, *vik-ro*, the action of which upon *yor-san* results in absolute annihilation of the *lor*. To give you an idea of what this means in terms of heat generation, and therefore power, let me remind you that if coal could be absolutely annihilated it would release eighteen thousand million times more energy than by ordinary combustion.

Thinking therefore in terms of heat rather than power, I designed a small balloon gas bag of tarel, that incredibly strong fabric woven from the web of the targo, which was to be carried, collapsed, in a small container from which it could be shot by a powerful spring. Simultaneously, an infinitesimal piece of *lor* was to be annihilated, instantaneously generating sufficient heat to inflate the balloon, and continuing to generate such heat for a considerable period of time.

Thus, the airman compelled to bail out could be sustained

in the air for a great length of time, or, by means of a rip cord, descend gradually to the ground. I was greatly disappointed that I could not have completed my experimental ballochute, as I called it.

But to get back to my narrative. As soon as the first anotar was completed I gave it a gruelling test. It was a sweet ship; but as I had incorporated some new ideas in its design, we felt it advisable to give it a cross-country test before Ero Shan set out on the long flight to Havatoo. Here is where either Fate or stupidity took a hand in shaping my destiny. This time I am going to give myself the benefit of the doubt and call it Fate.

We provisioned the ship for a long cruise, said our good-bys, and took off early one morning. I knew that Duare didn't want me to go by the expression in her eyes and the way she clung to me. I promised her that I would be back in not more than three days; and with her kisses still warm upon my lips, I climbed into the forward cockpit with Ero Shan and took off.

I had never flown very far west over Anlap, and as that part of the continent has never been thoroughly explored I decided to cruise in that direction and have a look at it. Sanara is at the extreme eastern end of Anlap, which, according to Amtorian maps, extends in a westerly direction for about three thousand miles. But as Amtorian maps are based upon an erroneous conception of the shape of the planet, I was sure that the distance was nearer six thousand miles than three thousand. Barring accidents, I felt that we should make the round trip in something like twenty-five hours flying at full speed; but as I wished to map the country roughly, we would have to fly much slower on the way out. However, I felt that three days would give us ample time. It would also be an adequate test flight for the anotar.

We passed over some very beautiful country the first day, and came down for the night in the center of a vast plain upon which there was no sign of human habitation and therefore no likelihood of our being attacked during the night. However, we took turns keeping watch.

When we awoke, the inner cloud envelope hung much lower than I had ever before seen it; and it was billowing up and down. I had never before seen it so agitated. However, we took off and continued on toward the west with a ceiling of about two thousand feet.

We had not flown far before I noticed that our compass was behaving most erratically. Though I knew that we were still flying due west, because of landmarks I had noted on our map the evening before, the compass indicated that we were flying south; and presently it gave up the ghost entirely, the needle swinging back and forth, sometimes a full three hundred and sixty degrees. And to make matters worse, the inner cloud envelope was dropping lower and lower. In less than half an hour our ceiling had fallen from two thousand to a thousand feet.

'This,' I said to Ero Shan, 'is the end of our test flight. I am going to turn back. We've mapped the country well enough to fly back to Sanara without any compass, but I certainly won't take the risk of flying on any farther with those clouds dropping lower and lower all the time and with no compass to guide us if they should eventually envelop us.'

'You're absolutely right,' agreed Ero Shan. 'Look at 'em now. They've dropped to within five hundred feet in the last fifteen minutes.'

'I'm going to land and wait it out as soon as we get beyond this forest,' I said.

We were flying over a considerable area of forest land where a forced landing would have meant a crackup, which, if we survived it, would mean a long walk of between five and six thousand miles back to Sanara through a savage wilderness inhabited by terrible beasts and, perhaps, even more terrible men. It was something we couldn't afford to risk. We must cross that forest before the clouds enveloped us.

With throttle wide we raced above that vast expanse of heliotrope and lavender foliage which, like a beautiful mantle of flowers across a casket, hid death beneath. And the clouds were settling lower and lower.

I estimated the height of the trees at about a hundred feet; and now, above the trees, we had a ceiling of about fifty feet. The forest stretched on interminably before us as far as the eye could reach. On the way out we had crossed this forest in fifteen minutes; so I realized that, flying without benefit of compass, our course was not due east and that we were probably now flying the long axis of the forest, either north or south. The indecision and suspense were maddening. I have seldom if ever felt so helpless. Here was a situation in which no amount of efficiency or intelligence could prevail against the blind, insensate forces of nature. I wished that Roy Chapman Andrews were there to tell me what to do.

'Here she comes!' exclaimed Ero Shan, as the clouds billowed down ahead of us to merge with the pastels of the tree tops, cutting our visibility to zero.

I said nothing. There was nothing to say, as I glanced back and saw the clouds settling rapidly behind us shutting off our vision in all directions; but I pulled the stick back and zoomed into that semi-liquid chaos. At fifteen thousand feet I felt that we would be safely above the giant forests that are occasionally found on Venus as well as above most of the mountain ranges. We would have, at least, time in which to think and plan.

Now I was flying blind, without a compass, over unknown terrain; than which there can be nothing more baffling to the human mind and ingenuity.

I turned to Ero Shan. 'Bail out, if you wish,' I said.

'Are you going to?' he asked.

'No,' I replied. 'Even if we landed without spraining an ankle, or breaking a leg, or getting killed, the chances of our ever reaching Sanara would be practically nil. The anotar is our only hope of salvation. I shall stick with it. I shall either live with it, or die with it.'

'I think it will be the latter,' said Ero Shan, with a grim laugh, 'but I'd rather take that chance with you than the other; though if you had elected to bail out I'd have gone with you.'

THREE

If Fate had been unkind to me in some respects, she had certainly not in the matter of a companion in misery. You'd have to scour two worlds to find a finer chap or a more loyal friend than Ero Shan, soldier-biologist of Havatoo. Soldier-biologist! In Amtorian it is Korgan Sentar, and it a title of high distinction.

We climbed rapidly, and at fifteen thousand feet we emerged into clear air with horizontal visibility limited only by the curve of the planet. Now we were between the inner and outer cloud envelopes. It was infinitely lighter and brighter here, but the air was hot and sticky. I knew that at night it would be very dark and cold, for I had dropped down through it that night that I had bailed out of my rocket ship before it crashed. What an experience that had been!

I hadn't the remotest idea of the direction in which I was flying, but I had the satisfaction of knowing that I could see mountains before I crashed into them. I flew on, hoping that there might come a break in the lower cloud envelope eventually that would permit me to come down again. I voiced this hope to Ero Shan.

'Such a thing might happen once or twice in a lifetime,' he replied. 'I imagine that the chances that it would happen to us right when we needed it are about one to several billion.'

'Well, I can always hope,' I said. 'I'm something of an optimist.' How much of an optimist I am, you may readily judge when I admit that I have been hopefully waiting for years for seven spades, vulnerable, doubled, and redoubled. I might also add that at such a time my partner and I have one game to our opponents' none, we having previously set them nineteen hundred; and are playing for a cent a point – notwithstanding the fact that I never play for more than a tenth. That, my friends, is optimism.

'Keep on hoping,' urged Ero Shan; 'it doesn't cost anything, and it's an excellent tonic for one's morale. Lovely scenery here,' he added.

'Ever been here before?' I asked.

'No; nor anyone else.'

'I have. It hasn't changed at all. There has been very little building activity since I passed through.'

Ero Shan grinned; then he pointed ahead. 'Look!' he said.

I had already seen. The inner cloud envelope was billowing up, gray and menacing. I nosed up to keep above it, and the first thing I knew the outer envelope billowed down and engulfed us. The two envelopes had met and merged.

What has taken such a short time to narrate really encompassed hours of flying. We might be thousands of miles from where we took off, or we might have been constantly circling and right back where we started from.

'How about bailing out now?' I asked. 'It is your last chance.'

'Why is it?'

'Because I am going down. The inner envelope has evidently risen: we have just seen it come up: the chances are that we have plenty of ceiling below it. If we hit a mountain, we die: if we stay here, we die.'

'If we don't hit a mountain, we live to die some other day,' cracked Ero Shan.

'Quite right,' I agreed. 'I am going down.'

'I am going with you.'

I came down in a long, slow glide – very slow: I was taking no unnecessary chances. Eleven thousand: ten thousand: nine thousand. I imagine that our visibility was something like a hundred feet, and at nine thousand I saw a jagged mountain peak looming dead ahead! I banked, and how I banked!

Ero Shan whistled. 'If your landing gear hadn't been retracted it would have scraped that mountain,' he said.

'It was retracted.' I felt as though my voice was pale: that had been a close call!

Now, in a new direction, I glided so slowly that most of the time I was almost on the point of stalling. Eight thousand feet: seven thousand. Six thousand: and Ero Shan and I both exclaimed in unison. Below us were hills and trees and rivers and – life!

The sudden reaction after that long nervous strain left us both mute for a time. It was Ero Shan who broke the silence. 'That doesn't look much like any country I've seen in Korva,' he said.

'Certainly not like anything I've seen near Sanara or Amtor and with which I am very familiar,' I agreed, 'nor is it like anything we flew over coming out.'

'It is beautiful,' said Ero Shan.

'Even Oklahoma would be beautiful after what we've been through,' I remarked.

'I have never been to Oklahoma,' said Ero Shan.

'Let's drop down and have a closer look,' I suggested.

It was a hilly country, cut by deep valleys and river gorges, a well watered country lush with vegetation; but it seemed uninhabited. However, we cruised around looking for a human being. I wanted to find one who was alone; so that we could come down and question him in safety. We had to learn where we were before we could make any plans for returning to Sanara.

Presently Ero Shan pointed and said, 'There's a building.'

It stood beside a river on a little knoll, and as I circled low above it I was astonished to see that it closely resembled the medieval castles of the Middle Ages in Europe. At least there were the outer walls with towers at the corners, the ballium, and the central building or donjon. There was no moat, and therefore no drawbridge, but the general effect was quite medieval.

While it was apparently in a fair state of repair, we saw no evidence of life anywhere about it; and so we flew on up the valley, where we presently discovered another similar edifice. This, too, seemed deserted.

'I wonder what's become of all the people,' said Ero Shan.

'They may have gone to a clam bake,' I suggested.

It so often happens that Ero Shan doesn't know what I am talking about that he had long since given up trying to find out. He says that what I refer to as a sense of humor would be diagnosed as psychopathy in Havatoo and lead to immediate destruction for the welfare of society in general and future generations in particular.

As we flew on up the valley we at last saw men. There were many of them, and they were armed. They appeared to be guarding a large herd of very small zaldars, about the size of earthly pigs. As the men were numerous and armed, we did not land; but continued on in our search for a single individual.

'Those zaldars looked very good,' said Ero Shan. 'I wouldn't mind having a nice zaldar roast right now.'

'Nor I,' I said. 'It is remarkable how good such silly looking creatures can taste.'

I really think that an Amtorian zaldar is about the silliest looking creature I ever saw. It has a large, foolish looking head, with big, oval eyes, and two long, pointed ears that stand perpetually erect as though the creature were always listening. It has no neck, and its body is all rounded curves: ideal for beef. Its hind legs resemble in shape those of a bear: its front legs are similar to an elephant's, though, of course, on a much smaller scale. Along its spine rises a single row of bristles. It has no tail and no neck, and from its snout depends a long tassel of hair. Its upper jaw is equipped with broad, shovel-like teeth, which protrude beyond its short, tiny lower jaw. Its skin is covered with short hair of a neutral mauve color with large patches of violet, which, especially when it is lying down, make it almost invisible against the pastel shades of Amtorian scenery. When it grazes it drops down on its knees and scrapes up the turf with its shovel-like teeth, and then draws it into its mouth with a broad tongue. It also has to kneel down when it drinks, because of its lack of a neck. There are two species of these animals: the large beef animal that is fully as large as a Hereford; and the smaller piglike creature, the specific name for which is neozaldar, or small zaldar.

The warriors guarding the herd over which we had passed had looked up at us in astonishment, and had fitted arrows to their bows as we came close. However, they had loosed not a single shaft. I imagine that the anotar looked altogether too formidable to them to risk antagonizing. What food for speculation and conversation we must have brought them! Even to the fourth and fifth generations their descendants will have to listen to it.

As we flew on I discovered a third castle perched on an eminence overlooking a river; and, as a forlorn hope, I circled slowly above it. Presently four people came out into the ballium and looked up at us. There were two men and two women. That didn't look very formidable; so I dropped down closer, whereupon one of the men shot an arrow at us; and he and one of the women screamed insults at us.

About all I could make out was, 'Go away, Morgas, or we'll kill you!' Realizing that it was a case of mistaken identity and knowing that I must in some way learn where we were, I decided to make an effort to allay their fears and win their confidence sufficiently to obtain the information we had to have if we were ever to reach Sanara.

I turned the controls over to Ero Shan; and, taking writing materials from one of the compartments, wrote a note explaining that we were strangers in their country, that we were lost, and that all we wished was information that would help us find our way home.

One of the men picked up the note after we had dropped it in the ballium; and I saw him read it carefully, after which he handed it to one of the women. The other man and woman pressed close and read it over her shoulder; then they all discussed it for several minutes while we circled around above them. Presently the older man beckoned us to come closer, at the same time making the sign of peace.

When we were as close to them as I could get without hitting the towers and they had examined us as closely as possible, one of them said, 'It is not Morgas; they are indeed strangers,' and then the older man said, 'You may come down. We will not harm you, if you come in peace.'

There was a small level piece of ground outside the castle walls, with barely space to land; but I made it, and a moment later Ero Shan and I stood outside the castle gate. We had stood there several minutes when a voice spoke to us from above. Looking up, we saw a man leaning from the window embrasure of one of the small towers that flanked the gateway.

'Who are you?' he demanded, 'and from where do you come?'

'This is Korgan Sentar Ero Shan of Havatoo,' I replied; 'and I am Carson of Venus, Tanjong of Korva.'

'You are sure you are not wizards?' he asked.

'Absolutely not,' I assured him; but his question made me wonder if we had, by ill chance, landed at an insane asylum.

'What is that thing that you came in?'

'An anotar.'

'If you are not wizards, how do you keep it up in the air? Why does it not fall? Is it alive?'

'It is not alive,' I told him, 'and it is only the pressure of the air on the under surface of the wings that keeps it up while it is in motion. If the motor that drives it should stop, it would have to come down. There is nothing mysterious about it at all.'

'You do not look like wizards,' he said, and then he drew back into the embrasure and disappeared.

We waited some more; and then the castle gate swung open, and as we looked in we saw fully fifty warriors waiting to receive us. It didn't look so good, and I hesitated.

'Don't be afraid,' urged the man, who had come down from the tower. 'If you are not wizards, and if you come in peace, you will not be harmed. My retainers are here only to protect us in the event you are not what you claim to be.'

FOUR

WELL, THAT SEEMED FAIR ENOUGH; so we went in. I was so anxious to know where we were that I didn't wait for any proper introductions, but asked immediately what country we were in.

'This is Gavo,' replied the man.

'Is it Anlap?' I asked.

'It is in Donuk,' he replied.

Donuk! Now, I had seen Donuk on Amtorian maps; and as near as I could recall it was at least ten thousand miles from Sanara and almost due west of Anlap. According to the maps, there was a considerable body of water separating the two land masses: one of the numerous great oceans of Venus. I was glad we hadn't bailed out, for the chances were that most of the time we had been flying above that ocean.

The older man touched my arm; and, indicating the older of the women, said, 'This is Noola, my woman.'

Noola was a wild eyed looking dame with dishevelled hair and a haunted expression. Suspicion was writ large on her countenance as she appraised us. She said nothing. The man then introduced his son, Endar, and his son's woman, Yonda, a pretty girl with frightened eyes.

'And I am Tovar,' said the older man, in concluding the introductions: 'I am a togan of the house of Pandar.'

Togan is something of a title of nobility, possibly analogous to baron. The literal translation of the word is high man. Tovar's real title, as head of the house of Pandar, was Vootogan, or First Togan: his son's title was Klootogan, or Second Togan. Noola's title was Vootoganja, and Yonda's, Klootoganja. We had landed among the nobility.

Tovar invited us into the castle, where, he said, he had an excellent map of Amtor that might aid us in returning to Sanara. While I had maps in the anotar; yet, as usual, I was always glad to examine new maps in the hope that I might eventually find one that was not almost entirely useless.

The interior of the main building, or donjon, was a bare and cheerless place. There were a few grass mats scattered about the floor, a long table, some wooden benches, and a low divan covered with the pelts of animals. On the walls were a few pictures, bows, quivers of arrows, spears, and swords. The arrangement of the weapons suggested that they were not there for ornamentation; but that this main hall of the castle was, in effect, an armory.

Noola sat down on a bench and glowered at us while Tovar brought out the map and spread it on the table. The map was no better than any of the others I had seen. While I was examining it, he summoned servants and ordered food brought. Endar and Yonda sat silently staring at us. The whole atmosphere of the place was one of constraint, suspicion, fear. The fear in Yonda's eyes was like something tangible that reached out and touched one's heart. Even Tovar, the only one of this strange quartet who had made any gesture of hospitality, was obviously nervous and ill at ease. He watched us constantly, and after he had put the map away, he sat on a bench and stared at us. No one said anything.

I could see Ero Shan fidgetting, and I knew that the situation was getting under his skin just as it was under mine. I tried to think of something to say to start a general conversation and relieve the tension; so I told them about our experience with the merging of the two cloud envelopes, and asked them if the clouds had come down to the ground in Gavo.

Tovar said, 'No.' That was his contribution to the conversation.

Yonda said, 'The clouds came very low.'

Noola, who up to this point had not entered the conversation, said, 'Shut up, you fool!' At that, the conversation languished and expired. Strangely enough, it was Noola who revived it. 'Nothing *human* ever went up into the clouds,' she said. 'A *wizard* might, but nothing *human*.'

Once again there was a long silence, while the servants

brought food and placed it on the table. Tovar said, 'Come and eat.'

The food was not very good: mostly vegetables, a little fruit, and some very tough meat which I thought I recognized as zorat meat. The zorat is the Amtorian horse.

I enjoy a little conversation with my meals; so I tried again. 'Who is this Morgas to whom you referred?' I asked.

They appeared a little surprised by the question. Noola 'Humphed!' and then elaborated upon this brilliant bit of repartee by adding: 'As though *you* don't know!'

'I am sorry to reveal my ignorance,' I said, 'but I really haven't the slightest idea who Morgas is. You must remember that I have never been to your country.'

'Humph!' said Noola.

Tovar cleared his throat and looked apologetically at Noola. 'Morgas is a wizard,' he said. 'He turns people into zaldars.' The others nodded their heads. Now I knew that they were all crazy; but after dinner they served in large tumblers something very similar to cognac, and I partially revised my estimate of them; at least I held my verdict in abeyance for the time being.

As I sipped my brandy, I sauntered around the hall looking at the pictures on the walls. They seemed to be chiefly family portraits, most of them very poorly executed. Noola was there, dour and sinister. So were the others, and there must have been fully a hundred that were probably of ancestors, for many of them were faded with age. I came upon one, though, that immediately arrested my attention: it was that of a very beautiful girl, and it was beautifully executed.

I could not restrain an exclamation of admiration. 'How lovely!' I said.

'That is our daughter, Vanaja,' said Tovar; and at the mention of her name, both he and Noola broke down and cried. Perhaps the cognac may have had something to do with this sudden access of sentiment: at least on Noola's part, for she had downed one entire tumblerful and started on the second.

'I am very sorry,' I hastened to say. 'I had no idea who she was, nor that she was dead.'

'She is not dead,' said Noola, between sobs. 'Would you like to meet her?' Whatever wizards there might have been about the place must have been contained in that brandy. While it hadn't turned Noola into a zaldar, it had certainly wrought an amazing change in her: her tone was almost cordial.

I saw that they would like to have me meet Vanaja; so, not wishing to offend them, I said that I should be delighted. After all, I reflected, it was not going to be much of an ordeal to meet such a gorgeous creature.

'Come with us,' said Noola; 'we will take you to Vanaja's apartments.'

She led the way out of the castle into the ballium, and we followed. Ero Shan, who was walking at my side, said, 'Be careful, Carson! Remember Duare!' Then he poked me in the ribs and grinned.

'And you'd better keep your mind on Nalte,' I counselled him.

'I shall try to,' he replied, 'but you'll have to admit that if Vanaja is half as lovely as her portrait it will be difficult for one to keep one's mind on anything but Vanaja.'

Noola led us to the rear of the castle, stopping at last in a far corner of the enclosure before a pen in which a small zaldar, about the size of a pig, was down on its knees gobbling a lavender mash from a trough.

The zaldar didn't even glance at us, but went on gobbling.

'This is Vanaja,' said Noola. 'Vanaja, this is Carson of Venus and Ero Shan of Havatoo.'

'She is very sad,' said Noola, sobbing. 'She is so sad that she refuses to talk.'

'How distressing!' I exclaimed, recalling that it is always best to humor those poor unfortunates who are the victims of mental disorders. 'I presume that this is the work of Morgas, the scoundrel.'

'Yes,' said Torvar; 'Morgas did it. She refused to be his mate; so he stole her, turned her into a zaldar, and returned her to us.'

Sadly we turned away and started back toward the castle. 'Could you keep your mind on Nalte?' I asked Ero Shan.

Ero Shan ignored my question, and turned to Tovar. 'Tell us something about this Morgas,' he said.

'Certainly,' replied our host. 'He is a powerful vootogan, whose stronghold is farther up the valley. He is a man of ill repute and ill deeds. He has powers that are beyond those of human men: he is a wizard. He has many warriors, and with them he attacked the other three castles in this part of the valley. Mine is impregnable; and we repulsed him, but he took the other two. Those of their inmates whom he did not kill, he took back to his own castle and turned into zaldars. If you would like to see his castle, I can show it to you from the south tower.'

I said that I would, and soon we were climbing the long spiral staircase that led to the summit of the south tower. Noola and the others accompanied us. Noola 'Humphed' a couple of times on the way up; and when Tovar finally pointed out Morgas's castle standing on an eminence and just visible far up the valley, she said, 'As though *they* had never seen it before!' I sighed, for I knew that the effects of Noola's brandy had worn off.

From the tower we could see a large herd of zaldars grazing beyond the river that flows below Tovar's castle. They were guarded by a number of warriors. It was, doubtless, the same herd above which Ero Shan and I had flown.

Tovar said, 'Do you see those zaldars?'

'They are not zaldars,' said Noola, 'as he very well knows: they are members of the Tolan and Ladja families to whom the two castles farther down the valley belong.'

Tovar sighed. 'Morgas turned them all into zaldars. We used to eat zaldars, but no more; we might be eating a friend or relative. Now we eat zorat meat – when we can get it. Very fine zaldars were raised in this valley: each family had its own herd, and we used to go down with our soldiers and steal the zaldars belonging to other families: it was excellent sport.

'As the best grazing is down at this end of the valley, Morgas used to send his herd down here; and he had a lot of them stolen; because the Tolans and the Ladjas or we Pandars would often join our forces and attack Morgas's men and steal his zaldars: we all hated Morgas. Although the rest of us stole each other's zaldars, we were good friends: our families visited back and forth and intermarried. Yonda is a Tolan and Noola is a Ladja.

'I'll tell you, those were the good old days; but when Morgas started turning people into zaldars, there was no use going down and stealing them, for no one would eat them: no one wanted to take a chance that he might be eating a father, a cousin, or even a mother-in-law. But Morgas and his people eat them: they are cannibals.'

It was almost dark when we returned to the great hall of the castle. Noola sat on a bench watching us with those wild eyes of hers: it seemed quite evident that she was mad. I was sure that Tovar was unbalanced, too; although he was not quite as crazy as Noola. I was not so sure as to Endar and Yonda: they sat silent and morose, and I gathered the impression that they were afraid of the others – that Yonda, especially, was: she had that frightened look in her eyes, which I had noticed from the first.

I thoroughly wished myself out of there, and regretted that I had not found an excuse to take off before dark. Now, with a few feeble, flickering lights, the castle was an eerie place; the evening meal something that might have been lifted bodily from a murder mystery story: the mad hostess, eyeing us with suspicion and hate; the uneasy host; the silent, frightened young people; the servants, slinking silently and furtively in and out of the shadows, terror and hatred in their eyes.

All these things conjured thoughts of poison, and when I had an opportunity I cautioned Ero Shan. We were both careful not to take food unless it was contained in a common bowl from which the members of the family helped themselves, and even then we did not taste it until after some of them had. As a social event, the dinner was not a success.

Immediately after dinner I suggested that we would like to retire, as we had had a hard day and wished to get an early start in the morning. At that, Noola laughed: I think a writer of horror stories would have called it a hollow laugh. I don't know what a hollow laugh is. I have never known. I should describe Noola's laugh as a graveyard laugh; which doesn't make much more sense than the other, but is more shivery.

Ero Shan and I had arisen, and now Tovar summoned a servant to show us to our room. We bade the family goodnight and started to follow the servant, and as we passed Yonda she arose and laid a hand on my arm.

'Carson of Venus,' she whispered, 'be – ' and then Noola darted forward and dragged her away.

'Fool!' she hissed at the girl. 'Would you be next?'

I hesitated a moment; and then, with a shrug, I followed

Ero Shan and the silent figure that preceded him into the shadows which the lighted taper that it carried seemed only to accentuate. I followed up creaking, rickety stairs to a balcony that encircled the great hall and into a room that opened onto the balcony.

Here, the servant lighted a small cresset and then almost ran from the room, his eyes popping with terror.

FIVE

'WHAT DO YOU MAKE OF IT ALL?' demanded Ero Shan, when we were alone. 'They all seem to be afraid of us.'

'Noola has gotten it into her mad mind that we are emissaries of Morgas, and she has evidently convinced the servants of this. Yonda doesn't believe it, and Tovar isn't sure: I don't know about Endar. I think that Yonda is the only perfectly sane member of the household.

'It all reminds me,' I continued, 'of a very old legend of the world of my birth. Among other things, it recounts the exploits of an old magician named Merlin, who could turn his enemies into members of the lower orders, such as pigs; just as Morgas is supposed to turn people into zaldars.

'Then there were a lot of brave knights who rode around the country rescuing beautiful damsels who were shut up in towers or had been turned into Poland China sows. There were Sir Galahad, Sir Gawain, Sir Lancelot, Sir Percival, and Sir Tristram, that I recall, who sallied forth on the slightest provocation or on none to rescue somebody; but right there the analogy ends, for there don't seem to be any brave knights here to rescue the fair damsels.'

Ero Shan yawned. '*We* are here,' he said with a grin. 'Now I am going to bed. I am very tired.'

The room in which we were seemed large because the faint light of the cresset, an emaciated, anaemic little light, lacked the stamina, or perhaps the fortitude, to travel outward to the four walls, which consequently seemed far away. There were two very low beds; a couple of benches, a chest of drawers: a poor room, poorly furnished: a dismal, gloomy room. But I went to bed in it and went to sleep almost immediately.

It must have been about midnight that I was awakened. In that dark room, it took me several seconds to orient myself: I couldn't recall where I was nor interpret the creaking noise that I could plainly hear. Presently I heard whispering voices, and then gradually I came to full awakefulness and a realization of where I was: the voices were just outside our door.

I got up and lighted the cresset, and by that time Ero Shan was awake and sitting up in bed. 'What is it?' he asked.

'They are outside our door,' I replied in a whisper. 'I do not like it.'

We listened, and presently we heard footsteps moving away. Whoever had been out there must either have heard our voices or seen the light shining under the door.

'Let's bolt the door,' said Ero Shan: 'we shall sleep better.'

There was a heavy wooden bar with which the door could be secured, and I quickly dropped it into place. I don't know why we hadn't done so before we retired. Then I blew out the cresset and returned to bed. Now, with a sense of security, we both must have fallen asleep immediately.

The next thing I knew I had what seemed like a whole regiment of soldiers on top of me: my arms and legs were pinioned: I was helpless. Nevertheless, I struggled; but it didn't get me anything but a punch on the jaw.

Pretty soon a light was made in the room, after which my antagonists bound my arms behind my back; then they got off of me, and I saw that Ero Shan had been similarly trussed up. About a dozen warriors and servants were in the room, and the four members of the family. Behind them I could see an open door: it was not the door I had so carefully bolted: it was another door in another part of the room: it had been hidden in the shadows.

'What is the meaning of this, Tovar?' I demanded.

It was Noola who answered my question. 'I know you,' she cackled; 'I have known you all along. You came to take us to Morgas in that magic ship that flies through the air: only a wizard could make such a ship as that.'

'Nonsense!' I said.

'No nonsense about it,' she retorted. 'I had a vision: a woman without a head came and told me that Vanaja wished to tell me something; so I went out and had a long talk with Vanaja. She told me! She told me that you were the same men who stole her and took her to Morgas.'

Yonda had come over and she was standing close to me. 'I tried to warn you,' she whispered. 'She is quite mad: you are in great danger.'

'If you wish to live,' cried Noola, 'restore Vanaja; make her a human being again.'

'But I can't,' I said; 'I am no wizard.'

'Then die!' screamed Noola. 'Take them out into the courtyard and kill them,' she ordered the warriors.

'That would be very dangerous,' said Yonda.

'Shut up, you fool!' shouted Noola.

'I will not shut up,' retorted Yonda. I had had no idea that the girl had so much spunk; she always looked so frightened. 'I will not shut up; because what you wish to do would endanger my life as well as yours. If these men are indeed the agents of Morgas, Morgas will be avenged if they are harmed.'

'That's right,' said Endar.

This made Noola pause and think. 'Do you believe that, too?' she asked Tovar.

'There would be great danger in it,' he said. 'I think that we should make them go away, but I do not think that we should kill them.'

Finally Noola gave in and ordered us expelled from the castle.

'Give us back our weapons and we will get into our anotar and fly away,' I said, 'nor will we ever return.'

'You cannot have your weapons, with which you might kill us,' objected Noola; 'nor can you have your foul, magic ship until Vanaja is restored to us.'

I tried to argue the point, but I got nowhere. 'Very well,' I said, 'if we have to leave it here, we'll have to leave it; but you're going to be very sorry that you didn't let us take it away, for some day someone is going to touch it.' I stopped right there and let her guess.

'Well,' she inquired presently, 'what if someone does touch it?'

'Oh, it won't hurt the anotar any,' I assured her; 'but whoever touches it will die.'

We were taken from the castle and started down the steep trail toward the valley, accompanied by admonitions never to return; but I had left a thought in every mind there that it might be wise to give the anotar a wide berth. I hoped that they would believe me: and why not? People who would believe that human beings could be turned into zaldars, would believe anything.

As we groped our way down to the floor of the valley our situation seemed rather hopeless. At the edge of the river we sat down to discuss our problem and wait for daylight.

'You and I are in a fix, Ero Shan,' I said: 'unarmed, friendless, and five thousand miles from Korva with no means of transportation across unknown and unmapped lands and at least once ocean.'

'Well,' he said, 'what are we going to do about it?'

'The first, and as far as we are concerned, the only consideration is to get the anotar back.'

'Of course, but how?'

'Rescue Vanaja and return her to her parents.'

'Excellent, Sir Galahad,' he applauded with a grin; 'but Vanaja is already in a pen behind their castle.'

'You don't believe that, Sir Gawain, do you?' I demanded.

'Of course not, but where is she?'

'If she is alive, Morgas must have her; therefore we go to Morgas.'

'Can it be possible that insanity is contagious!' exclaimed Ero Shan. 'If you are not crazy, just why would you contemplate placing yourself in the power of an insane criminal?'

'Becuase I do not think that Morgas is insane. As far as I have been able to judge, I should say that he is probably the only sane and intelligent person in the valley.'

'How do you arrive at such a conclusion as that?'

'It is quite simple,' I said. 'The other three families were stealing Morgas's zaldars. Morgas already had a reputation as a wizard; so, banking on that, he started this cock-and-bull story about turning their relatives into zaldars. Thereafter, no one would kill or eat a zaldar; so Morgas's herds were safe and he was able also to take over the abandoned herds of the others.'

Ero Shan thought this over for a while, and at last he admitted that I might be right. 'It's worth trying,' he said, 'for I can't think of any other way in which we can get the anotar.'

'Let's start then,' I said, 'there's no use waiting for daylight.'

SIX

WE FOLLOWED THE STREAM UP THE VALLEY, and shortly after daybreak we arrived before the massive gates of Morgas's castle. It was a formidable pile, frowning down from an elevation. We could see no sign of life about it: no sentry appeared upon the barbican. It was like a house of the dead.

I picked up a rock and pounded on the gates, and then I called aloud. 'He doesn't seem much afraid of an attack by enemies,' remarked Ero Shan.

'That is probably because he has no enemies left to attack him,' I suggested, as I continued to pound on the gates.

Presently a little wicket in the gate was opened and a pair of eyes looked out at us. 'Who are you? and what do you want here?' demanded a surly voice.

'We are visitors from a far country,' I replied, 'come to pay our respects to Vootogan Morgas.'

I saw the eyes looking past us. 'Where are your warriors?' demanded the voice.

'We are alone: we come in peace upon a peaceful visit.'

There was a pause, as though the voice were scratching its head in thought. 'Wait here,' it said, and slammed the wicket closed.

We waited fifteen minutes, during which men came onto the barbican above us and looked down at us and the wicket opened and closed several times and eyes stared at us; but no one spoke. Soon, however, the gates swung open; and an officer bade us enter. Behind, was a detachment of some twenty warriors.

'Vootogan Morgas will see you,' said the officer. He was looking us over carefully. 'You have no weapons?' he asked.

'None,' I assured him.

'Then come with me.'

The twenty warriors surrounded us as we crossed the ballium toward the donjon, a large circular building surrounded by a fosse in the bottom of which many sharpened stakes were embedded. To my amazement, I saw that the fosse was spanned by a drawbridge: Morgas was a jump ahead of his contemporaries.

We entered immediately into a large hall, at the far end of which a man was seated upon a very high dais. Warriors were banked behind him, and others were posted below the dais. In addition to these, there were probably a hundred people in the great hall: both men and women. I immediately looked for Vanaja, but I did not see her.

We were conducted to the foot of the steps leading up to the dais. The man, whom I assumed to be Morgas, looked us over carefully. He was a most unprepossessing person: his hair, growing low upon his forehead, stood up on end; the whites of his eyes showed all around the irises; and his eyes were set very close to his nose. His hands were extremely long fingered and slender: the kind of hands that, in a man, have always impressed me as being particularly revolting, almost obscene. His skin was an unhealthy white: it had a corpselike pallor. All in all, as you may have gathered, he was a most obnoxious appearing person.

The room was very quiet, there was not a sound, when suddenly he shouted, 'Silence! I cannot endure this infernal noise. Chop off their heads! Chop off their heads! Then, perhaps, I shall have peace.'

This was the first outward demonstration of his insanity that we had witnessed; though his appearance had immediately convinced me that he was a congenital maniac. The only reaction to his outburst was a babble of voices and stamping of feet.

'That is better,' he shouted above the din; 'now I can sleep. Put their heads back on again.' His eyes, which had been wandering about the hall, now returned to us. 'Who are you?' he demanded.

'These are the strangers from far countries who have come to visit you,' explained the officer who accompanied us.

'I am Vootogan Morgas, the wizard of Gavo,' said the man

on the dais. 'Who are you?'

'This is Korgan Sentar Ero Shan of Havatoo,' I replied, indicating my companion; 'and I am Carson of Venus, Tanjong of Korva.'

'So you don't believe I'm a wizard, eh?' demanded Morgas, and before we could make any reply, he added, 'Come up here, and I'll show you. Don't think I'm a wizard, eh! Don't think I'm a wizard, eh! Come up here! Come up here!'

It seemed wise to humor him: so we mounted the steps to the dais, where he was rummaging around in his pocket pouch for something. At last he found what he had been searching for, and withdrew a small nut, which he held up before us between a thumb and index finger.

'Here you see a small nut,' he announced. 'Here! take it; examine it.'

We took it and examined it. 'It is, indeed, a small nut,' said Ero Shan.

Morgas snatched it away from him, palmed it, rubbed his hands together, made some passes in the air, and then opened his hands. The nut had disappeared.

'Extraordinary!' I exclaimed.

Morgas seemed vastly pleased. 'Have you ever before seen wizardry like that?' he asked.

I thought it best to assure him that I never had.

'You've seen nothing,' he explained; then he approached Ero Shan and pretended to take the nut from one of his ears. The people in the hall gasped simultaneously. It was as spontaneous and unrehearsed as the drafting of a president for a third term.

'Amazing!' said Ero Shan.

After this Morgas did a few more parlor tricks of simple legerdemain. It was plain to see how he had commenced originally to get the idea that he was a wizard and to impress it on his simple and ignorant followers.

'Now,' he said, at last, 'I am going to show you something that will really take your breath away.' He looked around the hall, and presently fastened his eyes on an individual at the side of the room. 'You Ladjan,' he shouted; 'come here!' The man approached, fearfully, I thought. 'This is one of the members of the Ladja family,' Morgas explained to us. 'I have turned him into a zaldar. You are a zaldar, aren't you?' he demanded of the man. The fellow nodded. 'Then be a zaldar!' screamed Morgas, at which the poor creature went down on his hands and knees and scampered about the hall. 'Feed!' shouted Morgas, and the man put his face close to the earth floor and pretended to scrape up turf with his upper teeth.

'Feed!' shouted Morgas. 'I told you to feed: you are only pretending to feed. How do you expect to get fat enough to butcher, if you don't eat anything? Eat!'

The unfortunate creature now dug at the hard packed earth of the dirt floor with his upper teeth, letting the dirt drop from his mouth immediately. That made Morgas furious. 'Swallow it, zaldar!' he screamed; and the man, half choking, did as he was bid. 'There!' exclaimed Morgas, triumphantly. 'Now do you continue to deny that I am a wizard?'

'We have not denied it,' said Ero Shan.

'So! you call me a liar?' he demanded angrily.

I thought that we were in for it then; but his manner suddenly changed, as though he had entirely forgotten the imagined insult. 'How did you get here to Gavo?' he asked in a quiet, rational tone.

'We flew in in an anotar,' I explained, 'and came down to inquire where we were; because we were lost.'

'What is an anotar?' asked Morgas.

'A ship that flies in the air,' I replied.

'So they did not lie to me,' muttered the vootogan. 'My herdsmen told me of the strange thing that flew through the air, and I thought they were lying. You know how it is with herdsmen. They all lie. Where is this anotar?'

'One of your enemies has it; and if we don't get it back, he may use it to destroy you.'

'You mean Tovar? He is the only enemy I have left. How did he get the thing?'

I explained how we had been betrayed and overpowered. 'So we came to you to enlist your aid in recovering our anotar.'

'Impossible,' said Morgas; 'Tovar's stronghold is impregnable. I have tried many times to take it.'

'With the anotar and our r-ray pistols it could be taken,' I assured him.

'What are r-ray pistols? Where are they? Let me see them.'

'They are weapons that kill from a great distance. Tovar has them now. If he learns how to use them and the anotar, he can fly over here and kill you all.'

Morgas shook his head. 'No one can take Tovar's stronghold,' he said.

'That won't be necessary,' I explained. 'We can get the anotar and the pistols back without risking a single life.'

'How?' he demanded.

'By letting us return Vanaja to her parents,' I said.

Morgas's countenance clouded. 'What do you know about Vanaja?' he demanded.

'Only what Tovar and his woman told us.'

'They already have her,' snapped Morgas. 'She is a zaldar now. I sent her back to them a long time ago.'

'Such a good wizard as you should be able to turn a zaldar into Vanaja,' I suggested.

He looked at me narrowly. I think he suspected that I was spoofing him, but he came right back at me: 'Bring Vanaja from Tovar's stronghold and I will transform her into a girl again.' Then he stood up, yawned, and left the hall by a little doorway behind his throne.

Our interview with Morgas was ended.

SEVEN

ERO SHAN AND I left the Great Hall with Fadan, the officer who had brought us in. 'What now?' I asked him.

Fadan shrugged. 'He didn't order you destroyed or imprisoned,' he said: 'so I guess that you're safe for the time being. I'll find a place for you to sleep, and you can eat with the officers. If I were you, I'd keep out of sight as much as possible. Our vootogan is a little forgetful. If he doesn't see you, he may forget all about you; and those he forgets are the safest.'

After Fadan had shown us our quarters, he left us to our own devices after warning us again not to enter the main building, where we would be most likely to encounter Morgas.

'He seldom comes outside any more,' he added, 'so you are reasonably safe out here. And keep out of the garden,' he concluded. 'No one is allowed in there.'

'Well,' I said to Ero Shan when we were alone, 'are we prisoners or guests?'

'I think we could walk out almost any night we chose to,' he replied, 'you must have noticed that the gate was not manned when we arrived.'

'Yes, but I don't want to walk out as long as there is a chance that we may find Vanaja and take her with us. Without her we don't get the anotar back.'

'Do you think she's here?'

'I don't know, but I am inclined to believe that she is. Morgas may be crazy enough to believe his own foolish claims to wizardry, but I doubt if he really believes that he turned Vanaja into a zaldar. He just doesn't want to give her up: that's all, and if she's as good looking as that picture we saw, I don't blame him.'

'Perhaps she's dead,' suggested Ero Shan.

'We'll stick around until we find out.'

Morgas's castle was large, and in addition to the donjon there were a number of smaller buildings within the enclosure which must have comprised fully twenty acres. Here, in addition to his retainers and their families, were a couple of hundred prisoners, held by their fear of Morgas.

I came to the conclusion that the fellow had some hypnotic powers, but I doubted that his victims really thought that they were zaldars. They were just fearful of what their maniac master would do to them if they didn't play his game. He used these captives to cultivate his fields farther up the valley above the castle and to tend the herds of zaldars after they were brought in from pasture by the herdsmen. They all pretended to think that these zaldars were human beings transformed by Morgas's wizardry. Consequently they would not eat them. This left all the zaldar steaks for Morgas's people.

I tried to talk with several of these prisoners, both Tolans and Ladjas; but they seemed to fear me, probably because I was a stranger. They seemed hopelessly apathetic, accepting the fallacy that they were zaldars either because of fear of Morgas, or, as I came to believe, through self-hypnotism resulting from long suggestion. Some of them insisted that because they were zaldars they could not understand me; one or two even grunted like zaldars.

I discovered a couple who were willing to talk a little; but when I asked them about Vanaja they closed up like clams, their suspicions immediately aroused. Ero Shan and I came to the conclusion that there was some sort of special mystery surrounding the fate of Vanaja, and that made me all the more anxious to know the truth; aside from the possibility of using her to get the anotar back, I was commencing to take a definite personal interest in this girl whom I had never seen.

Ero Shan and I were constantly wandering around the enclosure, and though we saw many women among the prisoners there was none who even vaguely resembled the picture we had seen of Vanaja. After a week of this, we had about come to the conclusion that if Vanaja were one of Morgas's prisoners, he kept her shut up in the donjon – a really logical conclusion.

We saw Fadan nearly every day, and he continued to be very friendly; but when, one day, I asked him point blank what had become of Vanaja, he shook his head angrily. 'Ill considered curiosity is sometimes fatal,' he snapped: 'the vootogan has told you where Vanaja is; if I were you I wouldn't inquire any further.'

The conversation folded its tent like an Arab. I was squelched. Perhaps I shouldn't have brought the subject up in the presence of others. It was at the noon meal, and there were a number of officers present. After we had quit the mess hall, Fadan said, 'And don't forget what I told you about the garden. Keep out of it!'

'That,' I said to Ero Shan after Fadan had left us, 'was not said for nothing.'

'Of course it wasn't,' he agreed. 'It was said to keep us out of the garden and out of trouble.'

'I am not so sure. Anyway, it has had the opposite effect: I am going into the garden.'

'Once you told me of a very wise man of that world from which you came, who said, in effect, that only the stupid have adventures.'

'Quite right,' I said: 'I am stupid.'

'So am I,' said Ero Shan. 'I am going with you.'

'No. I am going alone. There is no reason why both of us should get into trouble. If I get in and you don't you might be able to help me; if we both get in there will be no one to help us.'

Ero Shan had to agree that I was right, and so I approached the garden gate alone. The garden is bounded on three sides by a high wall and on the fourth by the donjon. The gate was not latched, and I walked in and closed it after me. Mechanical locks are not needed in Morgas's stronghold. When he says keep out, that puts as effective a lock on a gate or door as any locksmith could contrive. Fear was the lock to which stupidity was the key. But was my act stupid? Only time would tell.

The garden was quite beautiful in a bizarre sort of way. It was such a garden as might have been conceived only by a mad mind, yet it was beautiful because of the natural beauty of flowers and trees and shrubs, which defy man to render them unbeautiful. Its walks were laid out in maze-like confusion, and I had gone only a short distance along them when I realized that I might have difficulty in finding my way out again; yet I ventured on, though I had no Ariadne to give me a clew of thread to guide me from the labyrinth. The only goddess upon whom I might rely was Lady Luck.

However, my power of orientation is excellent; and I felt that I might depend upon that by carefully noting every turn that I made. I soon had my mind filled with turns, all of which I would have to mentally reverse on my return trip to the gate.

Presently I came to an open space about fifty by a hundred feet in extent, and here I saw a woman walking with bowed head. Her back was toward me; and I could not see her face, but I immediately jumped to the conclusion that this was Vanaja; probably because I was in the garden for the pexress purpose of finding Vanaja.

I approached her slowly and when I was a few paces from her, I said in a low tone, 'Jodades!' It is a common Amtorian greeting. The girl stopped and turned about, and the instant that I saw her face I recognized it by the picture I had seen of the girl in the great hall in the stronghold of Tovar. This was Vanaja without a doubt; but the picture I had seen of her seemed now an out and out libel, so far more beautiful was the original.

'Jodades, Vanaja,' I said.

She shook her head. 'I am not Vanaja,' she said; 'I am only a poor little zaldar.' She looked at me dumbly and then turned and kept right on walking.

I overtook her and laid my hand gently on her arm. 'Wait, Vanaja,' I said; 'I want to talk with you.'

She turned again and looked at me. Her eyes were dull and uncomprehending. Morgas may be a wizard, I thought, or he may not; but he is most certainly a hypnotist of the first order. 'I am not Vanaja,' she repeated; 'I am only a poor little zaldar.'

'I have come from your home, Vanaja; I have seen Tovar and Noola and Endar and Yonda. They grieve for you and want you back.'

'I am a zaldar,' she said.

That thought was so thoroughly implanted in her mind that it was evidently her stock answer to nearly all questions or suggestions. I racked my brain in search of some avenue to her comprehension; and suddenly there flashed to my mind some of the teachings of Chand Kabi, the old East Indian mystic who had taught me so many things from his great store of occultism while, as a boy, I was tutored by him while my father was stationed in India.

I have practiced these powers but seldom, for I have the Anglo-Saxon's feeling of repugnance for anything that smacks of the black art; nor was I at all certain that I could accomplish anything with them in this instance in which I would have to combat the hypnosis which held the girl's mind in thrall; but I could try.

I led her to a bench at one side of the open space and bade her be seated. She seemed quite tractable, which in itself was a good omen. I sat down beside her and concentrated my thoughts upon that which I was determined she should see. I could feel the sweat standing upon my forehead as I strained to compel her, and presently the dullness passed from her eyes and she looked up wonderingly, her gaze apparently fixed upon something across the little clearing.

'Father!' she exclaimed, and rose and ran forward. She threw her arms around empty air, but I knew that she was in the embrace of the figment I had conjured from my brain. She talked excitedly for a moment, and then she said goodby tearfu ly and returned to the bench.

'You were right,' she said: 'I am Vanaja. Tovar, my father, has assured me of it. I wish that he might have remained, but he could not. However, he told me to trust you and to do whatever you said.'

'And you wish to return to your home?'

'Yes; oh, how much I wish to! But how?'

I had a plan, and I was just about to explain it to her when half a dozen men entered the clearing. At their head was Morgas!

EIGHT

THE WIZARD OF VENUS came storming across the clearing with his warriors at his heels. I could see that he was furious. 'What are you doing here?' he demanded.

'Admiring one of your zaldars,' I replied.

He gave me a skeptical look; and then a nasty, sneering smile replaced it. 'So you admire zaldars, do you? That is well, for you are about to become a zaldar;' then he fixed me with his terrible, maniacal eyes and made passes at me with his long slender fingers. 'You are a zaldar, you are a zaldar,' he kept repeating over and over again.

I waited to become a zaldar, but nothing happened.

His burning eyes bored into mine. I thought of Chand Kabi, and I wondered if this man did have sufficient power to make me believe that I was a zaldar. Chand Kabi could have done it, but he never used his great powers other than beneficently.

I pitted my mind against the mind of Morgas. At first I wondered, but presently I realized that I was immune to his most malevolent machinations. I did not become a zaldar.

'Now you are a zaldar,' he said at last. 'Get down on your hands and knees and feed!'

Then I made a mistake: I laughed at him. It wouldn't have done me any harm to admit that I was a zaldar in which event I should probably have been turned out to pasture and had something of freedom; but that laugh angered him, and he had the warriors drag me away and put me in a cell beneath the donjon, and for good measure he had Ero Shan thrown in with me.

I told Ero Shan of all that had occurred in the garden. He was much interested in this strange power that I had exercised over Vanaja, and I told him a great deal about Chand Kabi and my life in India. I told him of how my father used to go out tiger hunting on elephants, and I had to describe tigers and elephants to him. Ero Shan's imagination was intrigued. He said that he would like to go to India some day; which was, of course, quite impossible. And presently we feel asleep on the hard, stone floor of our cell.

We were there some time. A jailer came every day and brought us food. He had a most unprepossessing face – a face that one could never forget. It was burned indelibly into my consciousness.

Every day Morgas came and told us we were zaldars. He glared and made his passes, and at the end he would ask, 'Now you are zaldars, aren't you?'

'No,' I said, 'but you are a jackass.'

'What is a jackass?' he demanded.

'You,' I told him.

He smiled appreciatively. 'I suppose a jackass is a great person in your country,' he said.

'Many of them are in high places,' I assured him.

'But you are only zaldars,' he insisted. 'I know that you are just lying to me'; then he went away.

That evening, when our jailer came, he said, 'What fine zaldars! You are zaldars, aren't you, or do my eyes deceive me?'

'Perhaps they deceive you,' I told him, 'but mine don't deceive me. I know that you are not a zaldar.'

'Of course I'm not,' he said.

'Then what are you?' I asked.

'What am I? A human being, of course.'

'With that face? It is impossible.'

'What's the matter with my face?' he demanded angrily.

'Everything.'

He went out and slammed the door and turned the great key in the great lock almost venomously.

'Why do you always try to antagonize them?' asked Ero Shan.

'I suppose because I am bored. While they annoy me, they offer the only momentary escape from my boredom.'

'What is a jackass?' he asked. 'I know that it must be something obnoxious, or you would not have told Morgas that he was one.'

'On the contrary, the jackass is a really excellent fellow, a quite remarkable fellow. Creatures of far less intelligence have come to use him to – what should I say? personify? foolish stupidity. I am sorry that I called Morgas a jackass. I apologize to all jackasses.'

'You are a remarkable fellow,' said Ero Shan.

'Neatly put, Ero Shan.'

'I was just thinking that maybe you were a bit stupid in not using those marvelous powers you had from your Chand Kabi to frighten Morgas into releasing us.'

'There is an idea,' I said. 'It might be worth experimenting with, but I rather doubt that it will accomplish anything.'

'Try it tonight,' he said; 'people are more easily frightened at night.'

'Very well,' I agreed: 'tonight I shall frighten Morgas out of seven years' growth – maybe.'

'If you really made Vanaja think that she saw her father, you should be able to make Morgas think that he sees whatever you wish him to see.'

'Vanaja went and embraced her father and talked to him. It was a most touching reunion.'

'If I didn't know you so well,' said Ero Shan, 'I should be sure that you were lying. When are you going to start in on Morgas? That will prove to me whether – '

'I am a liar or a jackass or an A-1 Merlin,' I concluded for him.

'You are Galahad,' he said, grinning.

The great hall of the donjon was directly above our cell, and at night we could hear people walking around, and we could hear voices and, occasionally, laughter – not much real laughter; but, late at night, drunken laughter. I told Ero Shan that I would wait until things had quieted down and I was reasonably certain that Morgas had gone to bed before I started in on my necromancy.

It seemed to me that they caroused later than usual that night, but at last things quieted down. I waited about half an hour, during which time Ero Shan and I talked over old times in Havatoo; and then I told him that I was going to start in on Morgas.

'Just keep perfectly quiet,' I said, 'so as not to distract me, and we shall see what we shall see. It will probably be nothing.'

'I shall then be greatly disappointed and lose all faith in you,' he threatened me.

So I went to work on Vootogan Morgas, the Wizard of Venus. Although I didn't move, I worked until I was in a lather of perspiration. It is remarkable how similar the effects of sustained, highly concentrated mental activity are to those of physical exertion; but then, perhaps, they are due only to nervous reaction.

Ero Shan sat perfectly quiet. It was almost as though he did not even breathe. The minutes passed – tense minutes – and nothing happened. I fought to keep thoughts of failure from my mind. A quarter of an hour, and the silence of the tomb still reigned within the donjon. A half hour, but I would not give up.

Then suddenly we heard footsteps on the floor above us: the footsteps of running men and the shouts of men. I relaxed and wiped the perspiration from my forehead. 'I think it worked,' I said to Ero Shan.

'Something is happening up there,' he replied. 'I wonder what will happen next.'

'They will be down here in a moment, very hot and bothered,' I prophesied.

My prophesy was correct. A dozen armed men were presently at the door of our cell. It was unlocked and thrown open, and a torch was stuck in. Three warriors followed the torch inside and the others crowded in the doorway. When their eyes fell on me, surprise was written on their faces.

'What were you doing in Morgas's sleeping chamber?' one of them demanded.

'Doesn't Morgas know?' I countered.

'How did you get there? How did you get out of this cell? How did you get back into it?' The questions might have been shot from a tommy gun.

'Morgas, being a wizard also, should know that, too,' I told them.

They looked at me fearfully; they were worried and frightened as they talked among themselves: 'The door is heavily padlocked,' said one, 'and the padlock has not been tampered with'.

'It is incredible,' said another.

'Perhaps he does not realize that he is now a zaldar,' suggested a third.

'Could it be,' suggested a fourth in a whisper, 'that the vootogan drank too much wine this evening?'

'That does not account for it,' said the first warrior; 'because the woman who was in the vootogan's sleeping chamber saw what he saw, and she had not been drinking at all.'

So! I had wrought better than I knew, or else the woman had lied. However, the result was the same.

'Do not leave your cell again,' ordered one of the warriors. 'There will be armed men at every door, and if you come they will kill you'; then they went away, but before they closed the door I saw the ugly face of the jailer peering over their shoulders.

'Tell Morgas,' I shouted, 'that if he will release me and my companion and the girl, Vanaja, I will bother him no more.'

They did not answer.

'Do you think he will?' asked Ero Shan.

'I think he will,' I replied, 'but he will not know it.'

'What do you mean?'

'Wait and see.'

NINE

'YOU ARE REALLY a most remarkable fellow,' said Ero Shan, 'but I am commencing to be a little bit afraid of you,' he added, laughing.

'You needn't be,' I assured him, 'for Chand Kabi did not

teach me how to harm people physically with these occult powers. He, himself, knew how: he could have caused people at the farthest ends of the Earth to die had he chosen to do so, but he never did. Dear old Chand Kabi never harmed anyone.'

'Were I you I should experiment,' said Ero Shan. 'It might prove useful sometimes to be able to kill one's enemies at a distance. Why, you could win a whole war all by yourself.'

'I am content with what I am already able to accomplish,' I assured him; 'and now if you will devote yourself to meditation for a while, I shall go to work on our fine-feathered friend again.'

I did. Presently we heard a great commotion overhead. Thinly a voice reached us, screaming for help; and we distinctly heard the words, 'He is chasing me! He is chasing me!' There was a lot of running, and we could hear other sounds as of furniture being overturned; then, as I relaxed, things quieted down. I heard Ero Shan chuckle.

Once more the warriors came. They peeked in fearfully. 'You are here?' one demanded.

'Do you not see me?'

'But I just saw you up above chasing the vootogan. Why did you chase him?'

'Just for fun,' I said. 'It becomes very tiresome sitting here in this little cell.'

'You had better put your mind on other things,' snapped the warrior, 'for tomorrow you die. Morgas has had enough of you.'

'Well,' remarked Ero Shan after they had left, 'it was fun while it lasted; but you seem to have been blown up by your own bomb. What are you going to put your mind on now?'

'On Vanaja and the jailer. This may not be so successful as the other experiment, but I can only try. In the meantime, you may devote yourself to silent prayer.'

Ero Shan lapsed into silence, and I went to work on Vanaja and the jailer. I find it more conducive to success to have an accurate picture of my subject's face in my mind while I work on him. Nebulously hopeful, I had fixed the unattractive features of the jailer in my memory. They were easy to recall, but Vanaja's were easier and much more pleasant.

An hour had elapsed since I had had my last fun with Morgas, and the castle had quieted down again. It was so quiet that I could hear the approach of sandalled feet along the corridor outside our cell.

'He comes!' I said to Ero Shan.

'Who?' he asked.

'The jailer with the face of a Gila monster.'

The key turned in the lock and the door swung in. The underdone face of the jailer was poked in. He held a torch above his head.

'I am still here,' I said. 'If anyone has been chasing Morgas again, it was not I.'

'No one has been chasing Morgas again,' said the jailer, 'but I think he has gone crazy.'

'How so?'

'He has given orders that you are to be set free. If I were Morgas, I would have your head lopped off. You are a very dangerous person.'

'You are not Morgas,' I reminded him. 'What else did the vootogan order?' I knew, as I had given the orders myself; but I wanted to make certain that the fellow remembered them correctly.

'He ordered me to see that you and your companion and the woman, Vanaja, were put out of the castle immediately. The woman is waiting for you by the garden gate.'

'But suppose we don't wish to go?' I asked.

He looked at me in surprise, and so did Ero Shan. I was not trying to be funny. I just wished to fix his determination to get us out of there. I knew his type of mind: a small mind which a little authority inflated. Nothing now could prevail upon him to let us remain.

'I have my orders,' he said, 'I know what to do. If you do not go peaceably, you will be thrown out.'

'In that case we will go peaceably,' I said.

The jailer threw the door wide and stepped back. 'Come!' he ordered.

We followed him up and out into the ballium. Vanaja was waiting at the garden gate. 'You are going home,' I said to her.

'Yes,' she replied; 'I know. Morgas came and told me.' That would have surprised Morgas.

We followed the jailer to the main gates, which he unbolted and threw open. There were no guards there, as I had guessed there would not be, for there had been none the morning that we had arrived at the stronghold. Morgas was very sure of his power.

'Now get out,' snapped the jailer, 'and I hope that I never see your face again.'

'I have the same feeling about yours,' I assured him.

We three stepped out into the night and the gates closed behind us. We were free!

'It doesn't seem possible,' said Vanaja. 'I cannot yet understand why Morgas liberated us.'

'He will regret it in the morning,' I said, 'and we shall be pursued.' Knowing that Morgas knew nothing of all this, I knew that in the morning he would be furious when he discovered the trick that had been played on him.

'I should not like to be in that jailer's boots tomorrow morning,' said Ero Shan.

'Why?' asked Vanaja. 'He was only carrying out Morgas's orders.'

Ero Shan did not reply, and I thought it better not to explain. Had I, Vanaja would doubtless have immediately jumped to the conclusion that I was a wizard; and I had good reason to suspect that wizards might not be overly popular with the Pandar family.

As we proceeded down the valley in the direction of Tovar's castle, a change came over Vanaja which increased apparently in direct ratio to the distance we covered from the stronghold of Morgas. It was as though the spell of his influence over her became more attenuated the farther she was removed from him. Presently she was chatting gaily of her past experiences and trying to visualize the surprise of her people when they should see her returned safely to them.

'They may have difficulty in believing that it is you,' I said.

'Why?' she asked. 'I do not believe that I have changed that much since Morgas took me away.'

'It is not that,' I said. 'They think you are still at home.'

'How could they?'

'They have a zaldar in a pen behind the castle, which Morgas has convinced them is you. It may be a shock to your mother to discover that she has been lavishing affection upon a zaldar in the belief that it was her daughter. Your mother is not entirely – well.'

'What is the matter with her?' demanded the girl. 'She had never been ill a day in her life.'

'Lest you be shocked when you meet her, I might as well tell you now that her mind has evidently been affected – quite possibly by grief over your abduction and transformation into a zaldar. She really believes that zaldar is you.

'That is not strange,' replied Vanaja. 'Morgas has made hundreds of people believe the same thing. I believed it myself for a long time. Morgas can make people believe anything he wants them to believe.'

'He should be destroyed,' said Ero Shan.

'Yes,' said Vanaja. 'He is a terrible man. Frightful things happen in his castle. He has convinced himself that he has changed human beings into zaldars. Now he cannot tell them apart; so often men or women are butchered and eaten; because Morgas insists that they are zaldars. Nearly everyone there is so confused and terrified that they eat the flesh in the hope that Morgas may be right. Yes, he should be destroyed; but that is impossible. Morgas cannot be killed. He will live forever. He has said so.'

There was a finality in her tone which discouraged argument. It was evident that the spell which Morgas had cast upon the girl's mind and imagination had not been entirely cast out. It probably never would be while Morgas lived.

Our progress was very slow as we groped our way over the unfamiliar terrain through the darkness; and dawn caught us still far from Tovar's castle, for we had become lost during the night and gone in a wrong direction. We found that we had crossed the valley; and feeling certain that we should be pursued, we dared not risk going on by daylight.

We finally decided to hide during the day in one of the numerous little canyons which cut the hills along the valley's border; and after investigating a couple of them, we found one in which there was a little stream of pure water and a cave which we felt would afford a safe hiding place.

The canyon was a garden spot of trees, bushes, and flowers. We located and gathered a variety of edible nuts, fruits, and berries which we carried to our cave; then we settled down to pass away the daylight hours until darkness came again and we could continue our flight.

For safety's sake, Ero Shan and I took turns keeping watch

toward the mouth of the canyon. From the location of our cave, we could see up the valley a short distance in the direction of Morgas's stronghold; and toward the middle of the morning Ero Shan announced that a party of mounted men was approaching.

Vanaja and I joined him, keeping ourselves well hidden behind a large boulder. Coming down the valley were some twenty-five or thirty warriors mounted on zorats, those amazing creatures that serve as horses upon Venus.

'There's Morgas!' exclaimed Vanaja. 'See? He's riding at their head.'

It was indeed Morgas. I smiled to think of the fool's errand he had embarked upon and how chagrined he would be could he ever know how close he had been to those he sought.

I smiled too soon. Just opposite the mouth of our canyon, just when I thought that they would ride by, Morgas turned his mount directly toward us; and the whole party rode straight in our direction.

TEN

I AM NEVER CERTAIN that I shall obtain results from the exercise of that strange power which Chand Kabi taught me. Sometimes it fails. This may be due partially to the fact that I use it so seldom and partially to my own lack of confidence in myself. Chand Kabi used to say to me, 'You must *know*, my son, for knowledge is power.' He meant that I must *know* that I should succeed whenever I brought into play the mysterious mental force that he had taught me to develop.

As I saw Morgas and his followers approaching our hiding place, I cautioned Ero Shan and Vanaja to crouch down out of sight and remain very quiet; then I mobilized all of my mental resources and directed them upon Morgas. I seemed to know that they were speeding across the lessening distance that separated me from the object of my attack, concentrating into a pinpoint of irresistible suggestive force which bred into the ganglia of his brain that motivated his ocular perceptions and his power of volition.

I did not question that I should succeed in influencing him. I knew! But Morgas continued to ride toward us. He was so close now that I could see his eyes. I was certain that he could not see me, as I had adopted an age-old camouflage of the Indians of that far Southwest of my native land. Only my head from my eyes up were above the boulder which hid the rest of my body, and this was hidden from Morgas by the leafy branch of a shrub which I held before it.

Had I permitted myself to doubt, I should have been quite certain by this time that I had failed and that, unarmed and helpless as we were, we should soon be recaptured. And just then Morgas turned his head and looked back. Instantly he drew rein (a figure of speech, as zorats are ridden without bridles, being guided and controlled by pulling upon their long, pendulous ears).

'There he goes!' shouted Morgas, pointing down the valley.

Wheeling his mount, he dashed away, followed by his entire band. I had won! The reaction left me a trifle limp, for it had been a close call.

'They have gone,' I said to Ero Shan and Vanaja; 'but I think that we should go farther into the hills, as they may return.' I did not know how much longer I could lure Morgas upon that wild goose chase in which he thought that he saw me racing fleetly ahead of him. I grinned as I thought of his consternation as he contemplated my speed, which was swifter than that of his fastest zorat.

'What did he mean when he said, "There he goes!" ' asked Vanaja.

'He must have seen something,' I said. 'Perhaps he thought that he saw me.' Ero Shan smiled.

We went far up the canyon and climbed to the summit of a wooded hill from which we had a good view of the valley from perfect concealment. We could see Morgas and his men racing madly in pursuit of a figment.

'What are they chasing?' demanded Vanaja. 'I see nothing.'

I shook my head. 'Perhaps not,' I said, 'but Morgas sees something.' Then I thought that I would have a little fun at the expense of the great wizard. I caused the figment to zig-zag. Morgas and his men chased wildly this way and that. I led them up a rocky hill, from the summit of which the figment leaped over a cliff to the floor of the valley. The pursuers wheeled and dashed down again the way they had come. They found the figment sitting on a rock, waiting for them. I wish that I might have heard Morgas's remarks, but he was too far away.

As the party galloped toward the figment, it leaped to its feet and started across the valley, straight toward the river. I could see Morgas waving his arms and I knew that he was shouting commands to his men, for they suddenly spread out fan-wise in a pincer movement that would have the figment surrounded when it reached the river, which was, at this point, a couple of hundred feet wide and both deep and swift.

They were closing in on the figment when it leaped nimbly across the river! I guess that was too much for Morgas. He sat there with his men for a few minutes, staring at the quarry which had seated itself upon another rock across the river from them; then he turned and rode slowly back up the valley toward his stronghold. We watched them as they passed below our hill, puzzled and dejected.

'I don't understand it,' said Vanaja.

'Neither does Morgas,' said Ero Shan.

Although our recent pursuers no longer were a menace, we could not continue on toward the castle of Tovar, as Morgas's herdsmen were grazing their zaldars slowly down the valley. It would be necessary now to wait until night had fallen.

The remainder of the day dragged slowly for us. Late in the afternoon, we saw the herds returning up the valley; but we decided to wait until darkness had fallen before we ventured down from our hiding place. During the day, the spell of Morgas appeared to have entirely dissipated from Vanaja's mind. She became a normal and exceedingly likable girl, keenly interested in all that went on and quite courageous – a far cry from the fear ridden creature I had first met in the garden of Morgas. She continued to speculate with growing enthusiasm and excitement upon the reactions of her family when they realized that she was actually restored to them safe and unharmed. I, too, speculated upon this. I wondered what the reaction of the mad Noola would be. We had not long to wait.

Immediately darkness had fallen, we set out again for the castle of the Pandars. Within an hour we were pounding upon the massive gates. Presently a voice from within demanded to know who we were and what we wanted.

'Galahad returns with the beauteous princess,' Ero Shan whispered to me.

'Together with Sir Gawain, from the grim castle of the mad wizard of Amtor,' I added; and then, aloud: 'Ero Shan and Carson of Venus have brought Vanaja home.'

A head was protruding from an embrasure in one of the towers and a voice demanded: 'What's that you say? Vanaja is there?' It was Tovar.

The another voice and another head. 'They lie! It is the wizards! Kill them!' That was Noola.

'It is I, mother,' called Vanaja. 'These two have brought me back safely from the castle of Morgas.'

Noola's mad laughter rang out above us. 'You think that you can deceive Noola, do you? Well, you can't. I know where Vanaja is – she's safe in her apartments behind the castle. I have talked with her within the hour. Get out, all of you, before I have you killed.'

'But, mother, I am Vanaja,' insisted the girl. 'Let someone you trust come down and see me.'

'I trust no one,' screamed the old woman. 'Everyone is against me.'

'Then come down yourself and talk with me.'

Again that mad laughter. 'You think to lure me into the clutches of those two wizards, but I am too smart for all of you. Now get out of here!'

We could now hear Tovar, Endar, and Yonda arguing and pleading with the woman; but she evidently remained adamantine. Vanaja appealed to her father, but he replied that he must abide by the counsel of his wife. It was commencing to look hopeless.

'How about Chand Kabi?' asked Ero Shan in a low voice. 'He worked perfectly on Morgas; why not on the old woman?'

'I can try,' I said. I concentrated upon the mad mind of Noola, and presently an amazing thing happened. That which I had willed Noola alone to hear, I heard myself. Every one there heard it. A thin, squeaky voice from the ballium beyond the wall called, 'Noola! Noola!'

Those in the tower turned away from the embrasure I knew that they had heard that voice and had crossed to the opposite side of the tower to look down into the ballium. Then I heard Noola's voice: 'Why, Vanaja! How did you get out of your apartments, you naughty girl?'

In a squeaky grunt the answer came faintly to us: 'I am not Vanaja, you old fool. I am only a zaldar that Morgas sent here in order to deceive you. Vanaja is outside, waiting to get in.'

'Marvelous!' whispered Ero Shan. 'I am beginning to be afraid of you, myself.'

The 'old fool' got Noola. She was furious. 'How dare you, you dirty little runt!' she screamed. 'I have known all along that you were only a zaldar.' I had been certain that Noola would not relish being called an old fool.

It was only a matter of seconds before the gates were swung open and Vanaja was in the arms of her mother. With recognition and the return of her daughter, Noola's madness seemed to have passed. She was even quite cordial to Ero Shan and me. Tovar, Endar, and Yonda were delighted with the turn of events: two of their loved ones had been returned to them whole and unharmed.

The greetings over, Noola spoke to one of the servants, all of whom had gathered in the ballium by this time. 'Find that zaldar,' she said, 'and return the thing to its pen.' Then we all went into the great hall, we to recount, they to listen to, our adventures.

In a few minutes a servant entered. 'I could find the zaldar nowhere in the ballium,' he said; 'so I looked in its pen, and there it was, fast asleep. The gate was still locked and the pen was nowhere broken down.'

'That is very strange,' said Noola. 'We all distinctly saw her standing in the ballium and heard her speak to me, the impudent creature.'

'It is very strange,' I said.

'If she is going to act like that, I shall be afraid to have her around,' said Noola.

'Then why not have her butchered and eat her?' I suggested.

'That is an excellent idea,' said Tovar.

'Tomorrow we shall have zaldar steaks once more,' exclaimed Noola. The spell of Morgas had been broken – at least so far as the Pandar family was concerned. But there were those hundreds of other poor souls locked in his prison fortress, constantly filled with terror as they awaited death. There were the deserted castles and the stolen herds. There were these and other wrongs that cried out for vengeance. And above all was the horrid fear that lay upon this entire beautiful valley, which should have been a scene of peace and happiness.

Once again Ero Shan and I were escorted to the room in which we had spent a night of danger. Now we anticipated sleep in this same room without a single thought of apprehension. As we were preparing for bed, Ero Shan said, 'I have been thinking, Carson'.

'Yes?' I inquired, sleepily courteous.

'Yes,' he said. 'I have been thinking that in rescuing one girl and uniting one family we have made but a beginning. Would Sir Galahad and Sir Gawain have stopped there? Didn't you tell me that the Knights of the Round Table dedicated their lives to the righting of the wrongs of the oppressed?'

'Well, something like that, I guess. But if I recall my reading correctly, a victim of oppression usually had to have considerable pulchritude to arouse the chivalry of the noble knights.'

'Joking aside,' insisted Ero Shan, 'don't you think we should do something to rid the people of this valley of the terror that hangs over them?'

'I suppose you're right,' I agreed, stifling a yawn.

'This is the first time that I ever knew you to be callous to the suffering of others,' said Ero Shan a little curtly.

'I'm not,' I assured him; 'I'm just plain fagged out. To-morrow morning, Sir Gawain and Sir Galahad will sally forth to right the wrongs of the whole world. Good night!'

Ero Shan mumbled something that sounded very much like words that might have been translated into English: Go to hell!

ELEVEN

EARLY THE FOLLOWING MORNING I was up and out going over the anotar. There was no indication that it had been touched during our absence. Evidently my warning had been sufficient to protect it. I removed the compass and disassembled it, and much to my relief discovered that only a slight adjustment was necessary to correct the fault that had already cost us so dearly and might yet cost us infinitely more.

While I was replacing it, Ero Shan joined me. 'I suppose that we shall be off for Sanara immediately after breakfast,' he said.

'What?' I exclaimed, 'and leave this valley in the clutches of a madman? Ero Shan! I am surprised.'

He looked at me a moment, questioningly; then he shook his head. 'I suppose that is an example of Earthly humor,' he said. 'You took not the slightest interest in the valley last night.'

'On the contrary, I lay awake for fully an hour trying to plan how best to free those people whom Morgas has imprisoned.'

'And you have a plan?'

'It would be simple to fly over and shoot up the place,' I said, 'but that wouldn't be sporting. It would come pretty close to being plain murder, as they have no firearms.'

'And so –?' asked Ero Shan.

'Frankly, I have no plan that suits me. About the only thing I could think of was the spreading of a little propaganda among them to impress upon them the fact that Morgas is a fake; that he can't turn anyone into a zaldar and that what they should do is rise against him. After all, the people he has harmed are the one who should bring him to justice. We could drop notes among them carrying our message. We could even fly low enough to exhort them by word of mouth.'

'It will do no harm to try it,' said Ero Shan; so we set to work writing out our messages, a task in which we enlisted the services of the Pandar family and several of their servants.

Shortly after noon we took off in the anotar and flew up the valley to Morgas's castle. As we circled above it, we could plainly see the consternation we were causing. Ero Shan was at the controls, and as he circled low above the castle grounds, I dropped out our messages, each weighted with a small stone.

I saw a few brave souls venture from the hiding into which they had gone, pick up the notes, and scurry back again. Later, some of them came out and waved to us: the propaganda was having effect. Morgas emerged from the castle and made passes at us with his long fingers, evidently attempting to hypnotize us; but he remained close to the doorway. I think that he must have been rather fearful of the huge bird circling above him.

Well he might have been, for the antics of the anotar were awe inspiring. As we had flown up the valley from Tovar's castle, we had tossed about considerably, as the air was rough. Now, over Morgas's stronghold, it was even worse. A down draft would drop us suddenly perhaps a hundred feet, and we would bring up with a thud, as though we had struck a solid substance; then we might as suddenly shoot upward. Nor was the ship often on an even keel. Ero Shan was constantly fighting with the controls.

I was leaning far out over the side of the cockpit, dropping our propaganda leaflets and watching Morgas when Ero Shan banked steeply. Simultaneously a freak gust of wind caught the ship and turned it over. I fell out. I had neglected fastening my safety belt.

I have encountered numerous embarrassing moments in my career. This was another. Furthermore, in addition to being embarrassing, it might easily prove fatal. I was falling into the stronghold of a madman who probably felt that he had every reason to destroy me.

As I pulled the rip cord of my chute and floated gently down, I tried to plan against the immediate future after I had alighted. It was wasted effort. I could think of nothing, off hand, that might release me from my predicament. I didn't even have my r-ray pistol: it was in the plane with the rest of our armament.

Looking up, I could see Ero Shan circling overhead. I knew that he must be frantic. But what could he do? Glancing down, I saw that Morgas's retainers were scattering to give me a wide berth when I landed. Morgas was staying close to the doorway. It was evident that they held me in considerable respect. This gave me a ray of hope. Perhaps I could bluff my way out. Then a plan occurred to me. It did not seem like a very good plan, but it was the best that I could think of.

I alighted without falling. I was glad of that, as rolling about in the dirt would have added no dignity to my appearance and might have reduced my prestige. Peeking from doorways, windows, and around the corner of buildings and outhouses were the men and women whom Morgas held in thrall and his warriors. Unimpressed were a few score zaldars in the ballium. I was the only person there who knew whether they were zaldars or human beings. Even Morgas did not know, so thoroughly was his insane mind convinced of his power to transform human beings into beasts.

Turning my back on Morgas, I addressed the prisoners, or at least those whom I could see. 'You may come out of hiding,' I said. 'You need fear nothing from me. I have come to release you. My power is greater than that of Morgas. That you must realize, for how else would I have dared come down alone and unarmed into his stronghold?'

This seemed to make an impression on them, for slowly they came out and approached me. Morgas shouted to his warriors to seize me, but they hesitated; then I turned upon him.

'You are an impostor,' I accused. 'You have no power, otherwise you would not call upon your warriors to seize an unarmed man. If you are not an impostor, meet me single-handed.'

'You are a zaldar!' he screamed at me, making his riducu-lous passes.

'I am not a zaldar,' I said, 'nor are any of these people zaldars, nor are any of the zaldars human beings. You have not changed me into a zaldar; you cannot change me into a zaldar; you have never changed anyone into a zaldar.' I shouted this so that all might hear. 'Now I am going to show you what a real wizard can do.' I concentrated my thoughts upon Morgas. 'Look!' I shouted, pointing at the real zaldars which were huddled in a bunch at one side of the ballium. 'These poor creatures which you have used to destroy others will now destroy you.'

Presently Morgas's eyes went wide in horror. I alone knew

what he thought he was seeing – that which I was willing him to see. He was seeing those harmless, foolish little zaldars gradually being metamorphosed before his eyes into fierce and hideous tharbans – the ferocious lions of Amtor. He saw them creep toward him with bared fangs; then he turned and fled. Into his castle he dashed; but always behind him, roaring and growling, he heard the terrible beasts.

They followed him up the circular stairway to the top of the castle's loftiest tower. I saw him emerge at the very summit. He turned and looked back, screaming in terror; then he ran to the edge and jumped.

His broken body lay at my feet. I turned to the prisoners and the warriors. 'There is your wizard,' I said. 'He will never harm another. The prisoners are now free to return to their homes; and if any of Morgas's warriors think to prevent, I will cause his death as I have caused the death of his master.'

It was then that I learned that the warriors hated Morgas as much as his prisoners had, and were only held in his service by fear. One and all, they gathered about me; and there were tears in the eyes of many as they thanked me. I looked aloft for Ero Shan, but the anotar was nowhere in sight. I feared that he might have lost control and crashed; so I hastened toward the gates that I might go out and search for him.

As the gates swung open, Ero Shan leaped through the gateway, an r-ray pistol in each hand. He had made a landing near the castle and was coming to my rescue.

That night at Tovar's castle we had delicious zaldar steaks for dinner, and the next morning we took off for Sanara.

About PIRATE BLOOD:

When Edgar Rice Burroughs died in 1950, it was generally believed that all his written work had already been published. But, at the time of the reorganization of Edgar Rice Burroughs, Inc., in 1963, on the occasion of taking inventory of the office vaults, a number of original ERB works were discovered, none of which had ever been published. Among these were a number of short stories and novelettes, including *The Wizard of Venus*, and some novel-length works, of which the following, *Pirate Blood*, is one.

Pirate Blood was written, according to the author's notation on the first page of his manuscript, in 1932. It is shorter than the usual Burroughs novels and bears evidence thereby of being a first draft which was to have been expanded and filled out more – especially in the action-packed final half. Why Burroughs did not do so, why he set it aside to work on other tales and never to return to it, are things we shall never know.

By arrangement with Edgar Rice Burroughs, Inc., we are pleased to publish *Pirate Blood.* We think you will find lots of the good old Edgar Rice Burroughs zest and zing in the novel, even as it stands, and we think that ERB's millions of fans will greet it as an Earth adventure fully as exciting as those of Venus and Mars and other more alien worlds.

—DONALD A. WOLLHEIM

Pirate Blood

INTRODUCTION

THE FIRST HALF was drawing to a close. Neither team had scored. They were closely matched; so closely that the best-informed rather expected a scoreless tie. Johnny Laffitte at quarter, was running the Glenora team. The game was the last of the season, and it would decide the championship. Also, it was Laffitte's last game, for he would graduate in June. It was Johnny's big chance.

For three years he and Frank Adams had been fighting for the quarterback position. It had been a friendly rivalry but nonetheless seriously contended; but Frank seemed to get all the breaks. Johnny knew that in a pinch the coach always put Adams in, and he knew the coach was right; but he didn't know just why. And that troubled him. Everyone admitted that they were the two greatest quarters Glenora had never known.

Why was Adams just a shade better? Johnny Lafitte did not know, but he was out on the field today to prove that it was not so. It was Johnny's big chance.

Louis Lafitte, who repaired Glenora's old shoes in a little shop just off Main Street, was in the grandstand to watch his son in this last game. Henry Adams, small-town attorney, was there also to watch *his* son. Daisy Juke and Shirley Huntington were there to watch both the sons. Shirley was very much in love with Frank Adams, Daisy liked both the boys, and both boys were in love with Daisy. But Frank Adams got all the breaks; so when the four (who were much together) went places, Frank took Daisy, and Shirley and Johnny paired off; which wasn't so bad after all because they were very fond of one another, and the four always had a good time wherever they went.

'Only about two minutes left to play in this half,' remarked Billy Perry, who was sitting with the girls. 'He ought to kick.' It was Glenora's ball.

'What down is it?' asked Shirley.

'Third, and eight to go.'

The Glenora team was in a huddle; the ball lay squarely on their own thirty-yard line. The men came out of the huddle, took their positions, and shifted to the left; the ball was snapped. Lafitte took it and faded back.

'Cripes!' exclaimed Perry. 'He's goin' to pass!' They stood up; everyone in the stands stood; it was very quiet, as though the spectators had been suddenly stricken dumb.

Glenora's left half was racing down the field. He was in the clear; there was no Webster player near him. Lafitte had faded back to his own fifteen-yard line. Two Webster men were almost on top of him when he passed, but it was a perfect pass. And then, from out of nowhere, raced the Webster right end to intercept it. Before him was an almost clear field down which he streaked to a touchdown.

The Glenora coach dug a heel into the turf in front of the bench. 'Adams,' he directed, 'go in and send Lafitte out.'

At the beginning of the second half the score was six to nothing in favor of Webster, and Frank Adams was calling signals for Glenora. Never again that day was Glenora's goal seriously threatened, and in the fourth period a series of smart plays carried the ball to a touchdown. The Glenora fullback added the extra point that meant victory.

Four years had passed since that high school football game, and during the last three John Lafitte had sat on the sidelines during most of the important games that his college had played and watched Frank Adams steer the varsity to victory. The two men were still rated great quarters, but there was just that little difference between them that impelled the college coach to use Adams in pinches and against their stronger opponents.

The two men were still the best of friends; even their rivalry for the affections of Daisy Juke had not altered the friendly relations that had existed between them since they had entered grade school together. In spite of this and many other rivalries their friendship seemed to have strengthened during the years, and in their junior and senior years they had been roommates.

Adams was president of the student body and captain of

the debating team. He was a brilliant scholar. Lafitte had failed to make the debating team and had been defeated by a few votes in the election of class officers, now could he achieve better than passing grades on his way toward graduation; yet he felt no jealousy of Adams. On the contrary, he was very proud of him.

In a few things Lafitte excelled. He was boxing champion of the school and the crack shot of the R.O.T.C. unit. In addition to these, he made the highest grades in military science; but in his chosen field, law, he did not do so well.

Daisy Juke and Shirley Huntington and Billy Perry made up the remainder of the old high school crowd that had gone on to the university together. Daisy had been voted the prettiest girl and the most popular co-ed, but she was having difficulty in keeping her grades up to passing level.

'I guess I'm plain dumb,' she said.

'Too many dates,' opined Shirley.

The other girl shook her head. 'My people never amounted to anything. Dad's the best of the bunch, but he's only a poor farmer. He doesn't even believe in education. I shouldn't have gone beyond high school if it hadn't been for Mother. I got my looks from her, but I guess the rest of me's Juke.'

There was an embarrassed silence. Both girls were thinking of the same thing, for they had studied eugenics together. Shirley Huntington shot a quick glance at her chum. 'Don't be silly, Daisy; you can make yourself anything you want to be.'

The other girl examined her shapely, pointed nails critically. 'I wonder.'

John Lafitte was bending over a law book when Adams came in from class. He looked up and nodded; then he tilted his chair back and lighted a cigarette. 'The more I study law the more I understand why there are so many bum lawyers.'

Adams tossed his books onto his own desk, straddled a chair, and leaned his forearms across the back. 'You're studying too hard.'

'I know it; I'm pooped. But I wouldn't mind that if I were learning anything. I just don't seem to savvy.'

'Aw, you're all right; forget that inferiority complex. Gimme a Lucky.'

They smoked in silence for a moment. Presently Adams

looked up. 'I was sure sore about that election last night. If there wasn't such a bunch of nitwits in this class you'd have been elected.'

'Bill Perry's all right; he'll make a good president.'

'You got it all over him, Johnny.'

'He's a darn good speaker.'

'Yeah? Gab's all right if there're any brains back of it. Do you remember that guy who was student body president our freshman year, the one that circulated a petition and sent it to the President demanding that we recognize Soviet Russia? That's what I mean. That bird had won a national oratorical contest, and it went to his head where his brains ought to have been.'

Lafitte laughed. 'Billy's all right; he's not that bad.'

'Oh, I suppose not; but I still think you should have got it.'

'I don't seem to quite make the grade, ever.' Johnny snapped the stub of his cigarette into the fireplace. 'I guess it's the old Mendelian Law at work.'

'Nerts!' scoffed Adams.

'No "nerts" about it. Take your own family for instance: lawyers, writers, statesmen, diplomats, naturalists, astronomers, and two U.S. presidents; and Perry's is almost as good. Your blood can't help producing successes. But how about me? The only Lafitte in history was a pirate, and there isn't any great field for pirates nowadays.'

Adams grinned. 'You might try international banking.'

'Too ruthless for a self-respecting pirate.'

'And say, let me tell you something. You're all wet about Perry, and your theory falls down right there. I happen to know something about him. His father may be a respected banker from a fine old family, but his mother's people were not so hot. My father came from the same town she did. Her old man served a term for forgery, and she died in an insane asylum. But there's nothing wrong that way about Billy.'

'He's always inventing things,' suggested Lafitte, 'maybe that explains it.'

'I wouldn't mind being crazy like Edison. But on the level, Johnny, you don't believe in all this heredity bunk, do you?'

There was a note of sadness in Lafitte's voice as he replied. 'Yes, and so do you. Science may not be able to prove *how* it is done, but it certainly has proved that it *is* done – that germ cells carry certain characteristics down through a line for generation after generation, physical, mental, and moral.

'There's the famous Hapsburg lip, for example, that's come down through eighteen generations for more than six hundred years to King Alphonso of Spain; and the musical talent of the Bach family in which there have been twenty-eight famous musicians; the genius and talent of the Darwin family; and Commodore Perry's line, which includes twelve admirals.'

Adams grunted. 'It'd take a lot more than heredity to make an admiral out of Bill Perry; it's environment and training that count. No, it's all theory; and theories mostly don't work out. If a man believed the way you do, there'd be no incentive for him to try to make anything of himself. I won't believe it; it's rotten.'

'I'd rather not believe it, but I can't help it.'

'But think what it means to some people; it's ghastly. Think what it would mean to – ' He paused a moment, and then barely whispered the name, 'Daisy'.

'I have thought of her – more than of anyone else.'

Adams arose and walked to the window. 'It's a horrible theory; it takes all hope from life. What chance would she have with that blood line back of her – the blood of old Max Juke that has produced over twelve hundred physical, mental, and moral wrecks, paupers, prostitutes, thieves, murderers, and other criminals during the past two hundred years? I tell you it was environment that made those people the way they were. Her family got out of that environment; she's not contaminated.'

'I hope you're right, old man; but only time will tell; and maybe not in this generation.'

Chapter One

SPEED COP

EDUCATION IS ALL RIGHT, but there ought to be some way to pick out the ones who will be able to do something with an education after they get it instead of wasting a lot of time and money trying to make purses out of sows' ears.

I am a college graduate; but as far as I can see it has never done me any good, nor ever will. It hasn't even taught me the proper way to write my autobiography; so if it doesn't stack up with your preconceived notions of what an autobiography should be don't blame me – you shouldn't expect a sow's ear to write classical literature.

If you feel that you must blame someone, blame Mr McCulloch; it was he who persuaded me to attempt this unaccustomed and unpiratical task during a chance meeting in Singapore; so here goes.

There is nothing in my early life of sufficient interest to record. I lived in a small town; I went to the public schools; I worked my way through college. My father, Louis Lafitte, was a poor man, a cobbler. He was a good man. My mother was a good woman. They were happy together. Our home life was ideal; I look back upon it with only the happiest memories. I mention these facts to demonstrate that I was not influenced toward a life of lawlessness by education, training, or environment; there was absolutely nothing in my early life that remotely suggested that I might become a pirate.

My great-great-great-grandfather was Jean Lafitte, the French corsair of the Gulf of Mexico; between him and me lay a long line of respectable mediocrity.

As a boy I fell desperately in love with a little girl named Daisy Juke; but my best friend loved her, too. We all went to school and to college together, and as I felt that I didn't have a chance against Frank Adams I paired off with Shirley Huntington; we were almost engaged once. She was a peach of a girl.

During our senior year in college something happened in Glenora, the little town from which we all came, that worked a tremendous change in the lives of all of us. Our fathers were all in either poor or moderate circumstances. Even Billy Perry's father, who was the town banker, was far from being a Croesus. Frank's father was barely keeping one jump ahead of the sheriff by writing wills and drawing up deeds and bills of sale; once in a while he had a real case, but not often. Shirley's father was a real estate man, but that was slim pickings in those days. Old man Juke was a farmer and not a very good one; if he ever had a good year his profits all went to Billy Perry's father for interest; he tried raising a lot of things on his farm but could never raise the mortgage.

Then, bango! they struck oil on the Juke farm. That was the beginning of the great Glenora oil fields. In less than a year the town was full of millionaires. Frank Adam's father owned a farm that he'd had to take in lieu of money for a legal fee. As farm land it wasn't worth a whoop in Hades, but as oil land it made him rich. Huntington owned a subdivision where no one had ever bought a lot; he got rich. It seemed to me that everyone got rich except Dad; he kept right on half soling shoes.

I was studying law, but I had about two more years' work after I graduated from college before I could hope to pass the bar examination. Having no money, I had to find a job and study nights. Frank Adams's father got me on the police force, and I became what is vulgarly known as a motorcycle cop. I was a minion of the law. Outside of the pay, I liked it chiefly because I could wear a good-looking uniform and pack a gun. Lots of men are that way.

Right after the oil strike Billy Perry's father died, and the bank passed into other hands. The old man's estate wasn't nearly as large as had been supposed, and it sure looked like the hole in the doughnut compared to the new standards of wealth that had descended upon Glenora in a shower of oil.

Billy knew a lot about banking, and the new people put him in as cashier. I guess they thought, too, that his name would mean a lot to them; and it did. His old man was respected by everyone. I guess they didn't know about Billy's maternal granddad.

Billy had gone nuts on aeronautics. He'd built himself a big hangar just outside town and was working on a dirigible that was going to make him the Ford of the air some day. He figured on making a little blimp that he could turn out under mass production at a price of $563 F.O.B. Glenora, or something like that. He'd also designed a folding hangar and evolved a 'Hangar for Every Home' slogan. When his father died and he had to go to work he didn't have so much time to put in on the blimp, but I guess he worked on it Sundays and holidays.

It's funny what money does. All our lives a lot of us had been as thick as thieves; and then, all of a sudden, there was a chasm miles wide between me and the others; that was after we left college and I joined the force. They were all rich, and I was a cop. Nothing was ever said, of course, and they were always nice to me when I saw any of them. Perhaps I felt the difference more than they did, but it was there all right. I saw less and less of them at first; and then, after a while, I didn't see them at all.

At the end of two years I took my bar examination and failed. That was a bump. I guess I must have had ambitions; I had seen myself crawling up out of mediocrity and making a place for myself with the best of them. Of course I knew that I could take the examinations again, but something inside me had gone haywire. You can't plug and plug and hope and hope for years the way I had been doing and then get a jolt like that without something happening to whatever it is that drives a fellow on; I guess my drive shaft buckled.

I was sore on the world; so I took it out on traffic violators. This particular time happened to be a Saturday afternoon, bright and sunny; and there were a lot of them for me to take it out on. I'd been handing out tickets on the state highway just outside town until I almost had writer's cramp. I was sitting on my machine in a little hideout on a side road waiting for the next victim, when a great big, flashy roadster with the top down streaked by at about seventy.

By the time I'd wheeled onto the pavement and gotten under way it was out of sight around a curve a mile down the road; then I settled myself in the saddle and lit out after it. I thought to myself, 'This is going to cost you something, young fellow, whoever you are.'

The country club of the oil barons was about ten miles down the road, and I figured that that was just about where that bus was heading for; about the only people in town who drove cars like that were members of that country club. And I was right. The car was slowing down to make the turn into the entrance to the club grounds when I pulled up alongside and motioned it over to the side of the road.

As I left my machine and walked toward the side of the roadster I was reaching into my inside pocket for my book without looking up at the driver. When I did, I saw it was a girl.

'Why, Johnny Lafitte!' she cried. It was Daisy Juke.

I shoved my book back into my pocket; I wouldn't have given Daisy Juke a ticket if she'd run over my grandmother. 'I hope I haven't made you miss the train, Daisy,' I said.

She laughed and lighted a cigarette. 'I'm awful sorry, Johnny; it's new, and I wanted to see what it would do.'

'Did you find out?'

'I got up to ninety once, but that's confidential; don't tell anyone.' She was smiling all the time in that way she had, and all the old feeling I'd had for her ever since I was a kid broke out all over me like measles.

I came up and leaned on the side of the car and smiled back at her. 'I don't intend to tell anyone, but don't do it again, please. You'll kill yourself or someone else.'

'Where in the world do you keep yourself, Johnny? Why don't you come and see a fellow? I've often wondered why.'

'You've thought about me?' I asked.

'Lots, Johnny,' and there was something in the way she said it – well, I can't explain what I mean.

Her face was flushed, her blonde hair blown every which way; she was the most beautiful picture that day that I had ever seen before or have ever seen since; but though I was leaning close to her, my heart full of love, she was a thousand miles away from me – the chassis of the car she drove cost sixteen thousand dollars without any body, and I was only a dumb copper who had just flunked the bar exams; perhaps you know what I mean.

'Do you ever see Frank or Shirley or Billy?' I asked.

'Often.' She paused. 'Haven't you heard?'

'Heard what?'

'I'll whisper it to you.' She leaned close to me; I caught a faint odor of liquor on her breath. 'Frank and I are going to be married next month.'

I don't know which hurt me the worst, what she told me or the liquor. I don't remember now what I said after that; probably I congratulated her and wished them happiness. I know she asked me to come and see her, and I promised that I would; then she started up and turned up the driveway of the country club – where I could only go as a cop. I didn't write any more tickets that day.

Chapter Two

A MILLION IN LOOT

WHEN I REPORTED for duty at the station the next morning the captain called me into his office. 'You know Perry, don't you, the cashier of the Glenora National?'

'Sure.'

'We just got a call from the president of the bank; I just hung up as you came in. For some reason they have been suspicious about Perry, and two or three of them went to the bank this morning, figuring Perry wouldn't be there on a Sunday, to have a look around. The place has been cleaned: nearly a million in negotiable securities, gold and currency gone. They tell me he's been building an airship, and they got a hunch he's going to try to make his getaway in that. The cruisers are all out, but just as soon as one of 'em calls in I'll send it down to his hangar. In the meantime you beat it down there and make the pinch if he hasn't got away, and hold him till the car gets there.'

'How about a warrant?'

'To hell with a warrant; beat it!'

'O.K. chief.'

Here was a job I didn't have any stomach for, arresting an old friend like Billy Perry; but a cop's a cop and he can't always be as choosy about whom he arrests as I had been the day before when Daisy burned up the concrete.

Before I got to Billy's hangar I saw that he hadn't gotten away yet. A tiny little blimp was outside the hangar, and there was a little crowd, mostly boys, hanging around watching. Billy was on the ground when I pulled up; he hadn't see me coming; but when he happened to look up and saw the uniform, he went white.

He didn't recognize me then, and he didn't wait to look again. He just jumped through the open doorway of the gondola and tried to close it after him. It was a sliding door, and it stuck. Before he could get it to work I was inside with him. Then he turned and faced me. His eyes appeared strange to me; there was fear in them and something else, too – something terrible. It was just a suggestion of something that I seemed to glimpse in passing.

Then he recognized me and his expression altered. 'Why, hello, Lafitte! Come down to have a look at the flying flivver?'

In the distance, approaching, I heard the wail of a cruiser's siren. He heard it, too; I saw his glance dart through the window in the direction of the sound.

I shook my head. 'I came after you, Billy.'

'Me!' He pretended great surprise.

'I'm sorry, Billy. Will you come along quietly with me?' I couldn't be hard-boiled with a fellow I'd known all my life and played with as a kid.

Again his expression changed, and I saw that thing in his eyes; but his words disarmed me. Nearer now, the siren screeched through the streets of Glenora.

Perry shrugged. 'All right, Johnny. But you've never seen the wind-blown Ford; come and take a look at her before we go.' He turned toward a small compartment in the forward end of the gondola. 'Here's the control room.'

I glanced through a window and saw the cruiser turning into the field toward the hangar; then I followed Perry into the control room. 'Not much to it, is there?' he remarked. He laid a hand upon a lever. 'This,' he said, 'is an invention of mine.' He pushed it forward.

'What is it?' I asked.

'The mooring release.' He commenced to laugh. Then I heard men shouting, and again I looked through a window;

I saw the crew of the cruiser running toward us, shouting. And I saw something else; I saw that already we were above them – we were rising – and I knew that Perry had tricked me.

I whipped out my gun and leveled it at him. 'Bring her down!' I snapped; but he only laughed. There was a strange note in his laughter that sort of chilled me.

'Shoot and be damned!' he cried, 'but if you do, you're as good as dead. You don't know how to handle her; you could never ground her.'

I knew that he was right, and I saw that I could not bluff him. I slipped my gun back into its holster and turned back into the main cabin. The door of the gondola was still open and I crossed to it. Leaning out, I called down to the officers below, telling them what had happened. Then, without warning, Perry attacked me from the rear; he hurled himself against me, trying to push me through the doorway. I don't know why he didn't succeed; I thought I was gone, but I clung desperately to the frame of the doorway. He was pushing hard against the small of my back; then his feet slipped, and he went to his knees. That was all that saved my life.

I leaped to one side as he scrambled to his feet and charged me again; but I had had time to draw my gun, and as he closed with me I struck him across the left temple with the barrel. He dropped like a log. Behind him, against the far wall of the cabin, I saw several pieces of luggage: three suitcases and two big Gladstones. Without opening them, I knew that they contained the swag.

Again I glanced down from the doorway. It was a quiet morning, with little or no wind, and we had risen almost vertically. I guess we must have been about four or five hundred feet above the ground by this time. I could see the crowd, with the officers, standing craning their necks upward. Then I got an idea.

Stepping over the unconscious Perry, I crossed the tiny cabin and seized a couple of the suitcases and carried them to the doorway. Looking out again, I saw some of the crowd that had been following the ship almost directly beneath.

'Look out below!' I yelled. I don't know whether they understood what I said or not; then I dropped the two suitcases overboard. A moment later I heaved the other suitcase and the two Gladstones after them. I might never bring my prisoner back, but I had returned what he had stolen.

As I looked out again I had the unique experience of seeing a million dollars scattered over a couple of acres of ground. I saw the officers and the crowd running hither and thither gathering up securities, currency, and coin; then I closed the door so that Perry wouldn't be tempted to try to push me through it again when he regained consciousness and turned my attention to him where he lay sprawled on the floor.

He was only stunned and soon regained consciousness. I helped him to his feet and into a chair. He held on to his head, which I guess was aching pretty badly.

'Now Perry,' I said, 'when you feel a little better get busy and bring this boat back to earth.'

'And go to the pen? Not on your life! I've got a million dollars aboard, and I'm going somewhere where there's no extradition treaty and take it easy the rest of my life; and you're going with me – you can't help yourself. If you behave I'll split a part of the million with you.'

'You haven't got a million,' I told him.

'The hell I haven't! What makes you think so?'

'Because I just threw it overboard; it's probably on its way back to the bank right now.'

He took one look at where his bags had been sitting, and then he let out a yell like somebody's knifed him. What he called me I wouldn't want to put in anybody's biography, not even a pirate's. After he'd finished he seemed to feel a little bit better.

'Better bring her down now,' I suggested. 'As long as they got the swag back they may let you off easy. Maybe they won't do anything to you on account of your father's name and the reputation of the bank.'

He got up slowly and walked into the control room. The machine was what I think is called a pusher type; the motor and propeller were at the stern. The controls, however, were all forward. He started the engine, and right off we began to make headway; but instead of coming down I saw that we were making altitude, and he wasn't turning her back toward the landing field.

'Where you going?' I demanded.

'For a little ride.'

'Bring her down, Billy; it'll be better for you in the end.'

'And go to the pen? Not on your life.'

Glenora is about twenty miles from the coast, which swings in a southeasterly direction from Point Conception so that the southwesterly direction he was heading was the shortest route to the ocean. We were headed out across the San Fernando Valley toward the Santa Monica Mountains; after we crossed those we'd be out over the ocean. I realized that if I were going to do anything I'd have to do it in a hurry. I couldn't tell by looking down what speed we were making, but I guessed that perhaps forty miles an hour would hit pretty close to it; that didn't leave me much time. Pretty soon however I realized that it was just as good as a week, for there wasn't anything that I could do. Perry sure had me to rights; I was being taken for a ride, and no joke. I never felt so helpless in my life as I did then. I could have slipped the bracelets on Perry easy enough; but that wouldn't have helped me out any, for I couldn't navigate the ship. All I could do was sit tight and hope that he'd bring her down sometime somewhere.

We crossed the mountains and hit Santa Monica just below the old soldiers' home at Sawtelle, and there, ahead of us, stretched the Pacific. It was a fine, clear day; I could see Santa Catalina and far San Clemente lying like emerald jewels in a setting of turquoise. I recall even now that the beauty of the scene impressed me even through the pall of my anxiety.

Just as we were crossing the far-stretching strip of sandy beach bordered by the restless, wavering line of white surf I saw a land plane overhauling us; it was a Los Angeles police ship. It circled us and then came up close again on our port side. I saw the pilot and another officer in the cockpit and waved to them. One of them pointed down emphatically. I knew he was signaling us to land. All I could do was raise my palms in a gesture of helplessness.

Pretty soon two more planes joined the pursuit; these were civilian planes come up to see the fun. They couldn't do anything; neither could the police plane. Of course Perry had seen them, and he was chuckling to himself. It was evident that the Glenora police had telephoned Los Angeles for help, and those boys did their best to help us. The civilian planes followed us about halfway to Catalina and then turned back; of course, like the police ship, they were land planes.

After we had passed Catalina several miles to the northwest of it, I thought the other plane would turn back; but they kept right on. I imagine they figured that Perry was planning on landing on one of the other islands after he'd shaken them off, perhaps San Clemente or one of those off Santa Barbara like Santa Cruz; but after they'd got out fifty miles, and Perry wasn't heading for any island on that side of the Pacific, they turned back. It sure seemed lonesome way up there after they had left.

Perry hadn't said a word all this time; now he turned to me with a grin. 'Not many bank robbers get a police escort while they're making their getaway.'

'Isn't it about time to turn back?' I suggested.

'I'm not going to turn back.'

'Where in hell do you think you're going, then?'

'Quite a way.'

'To Honolulu?'

'And then some.'

'This thing wouldn't get halfway even to Honolulu; you'll end up by falling into the sea and drowning both of us.'

'Not much loss – a bank robber and a lousy cop; but we won't fall into the sea. I knew what I was doing when I built this flying Lizzie. I designed the motor myself to burn a fuel of my own invention; I've been planning on this for a long time, and so I happen to know that the northeast trades blow pretty steadily this time of year; that'll conserve a lot of our fuel. Eventually they'd blow us where I want to go, or pretty close, without any fuel.'

'Where's that?'

'There are about a million islands in the triangle formed by Sumatra, New Guinea, and the Philippines; most any of them will suit me better than sunny southern Cal.'

'But you can't ever reach there in this thing. Do you know how far it is?'

'About seven thousand miles.'

'For the love of Mike, Perry, turn around and go back while we've got a chance.'

'I'm not going back, and don't forget that I didn't invite you to come along; I don't want you along. If you aren't satisfied, there's the door; you can step out and walk back home.'

'What are you going to use for food on this trip?'

'I have plenty of food for myself, a month's supply; but now that you're along that will cut us down to about two weeks.'

'After which we'll starve to death, if we're not drowned first.'

'We'll be down on our island in two weeks.'

'How do you figure that out?'

'With a pencil – try it. Of course she's not built for speed. She can make sixty, but her most economical cruising speed is forty – that's 960 miles a day; divide that into seven thousand and you'll get seven plus. The trade wind is going to help us, too; but I figure on drifting while I sleep. Taking everything into consideration two weeks is a conservative estimate.'

'I hope you're right.'

He looked at me with that funny light in his eyes again. 'I am always right.'

'You and God.'

At that his anger flared suddenly. 'If you didn't have that gun on I'd fling you overboard, but I'll get you yet.' Then he commenced muttering to himself, and I thought I caught the words, 'You can't stay awake for two weeks'.

In an hour or so he seemed to have forgotten his sudden rage and suggested that we eat. That suited me all right, as almost anything would have that suggested a break in the monotony. The idea of sailing over that vast expanse of sullen water for weeks without seeing anything else was commencing to get me already.

The day seemed endless, but at last it passed and night came; then Perry shut off the engine and we let down the two folding cots in the cabin and turned in. I was tired doing nothing and fell right asleep. I must have slept like a log; but something awoke me shortly after midnight – awoke me with a start – and when I opened my eyes there was Perry standing over me.

Chapter Three

ABOVE THE PACIFIC

HE WAS HOLDING something in his hand.

'What do you want, Perry?' I asked sharply.

At that he commenced to laugh. I call it a laugh, but it was a sound that raised gooseflesh all over me; and I never was exactly what might be called squeamish. He walked back to his cot and sat on the edge of it, still laughing.

Something told me I wasn't going to sleep much more that night; so I got up. As I did so I happened to glance out a window, and what I saw gave me another start. It was a moonlight night; everything was plainly visible, and I saw the surface of the ocean rolling in great swells right there under my nose – we were only a few yards above it.

'Look out the window, Perry,' I said.

He just kept his eyes on me; they hadn't left me since I had caught him standing there above me. 'You think you're smart, don't you?' he jeered. 'But you're not as smart as I am, you dumb cop. I know your game; if I look away you'll jump on me.'

'I'd jump on you anyway, if I wanted to, Perry. If you don't want to go swimming, you'd better get busy, for we're almost in the water now.'

Then he took his eyes off me and glanced out the window. Instantly he leaped to his feet and ran into the control room. He turned a valve that dumped some water ballast, and then he started the motor. As soon as we were under way, he had no difficulty rising.

The cause of our descent was obvious enough; in the chill of the night air the gas in the bag had contracted, losing buoyancy. I realized that this was something that must occur every night and necessitate one of us constantly remaining on watch. I broached the suggestion to Perry.

When he replied he appeared more normal. 'We'll have to do something,' he admitted. 'I neglected to take this factor into account, nor did I figure on your weight either. If I wasn't afraid you'd turn back, we'd take turns at the controls and keep under way all night; at thirty miles an hour this motor could run forever, and as long as we're moving we can keep altitude.'

I was convinced by this time that Perry would never consent to turn back, and though I doubted the ability of the frail craft to cross the Pacific I realized that in the attempt lay our only chance for escape from a watery grave. If I ran east while I was at the controls and Perry ran west during his trick we'd never get anywhere, and so my reply was governed by these deductions.

'I won't turn back, Perry,' I assured him.

'How do I know I can trust you?' he questioned suspiciously.

'You ought to know; you've known me all my life.'

'That's right,' he admitted. 'I never knew you to break your word. Will you give it to me now that you'll keep the course I tell you to while you are at the controls?'

'Certainly; it's the only chance I have of getting out of this alive, and a mighty slim chance at that.'

'Come here, and I'll show you all you need to know; in an emergency you can always wake me up if I'm asleep.'

'Now you've got to do a little promising,' I said.

'What do you mean?'

'You've had it in your head to kill me. You've got to promise to lay off that stuff; I can't handle the controls and watch you out of the back of my head; and I've got to get a little sleep, too.'

That strange light came into his eyes again. 'Don't worry,' he said as suavely as you please. 'I was a little sore at first, but I've gotten over that. You'll be perfectly safe as far as I'm concerned.'

Perhaps he trusted me, but I wasn't any too sure of him. 'It wouldn't pay you to kill me now, anyway,' I reminded him; 'you need me. If anything happened to me, you'd go into the sea some night while you were asleep.'

He smiled condescendingly. 'That would be true of an ordinary man, but I am no ordinary man. Napoleon required but four hours sleep a day; if it were necessary, I could do without any sleep, indefinitely.'

So that was that; there remained nothing further to discuss on that score. But it certainly didn't improve my position. If he believed that he didn't need me he might easily grasp the first opportunity to rid himself of me, for both the additional weight that I represented as well as the fact that I consumed both food and water constituted me a definite menace to his own safety. I determined to watch him carefully and sleep lightly.

For the following several days nothing eventful occurred; the motor plugged right along and the northeast trades helped us on our way. Perry was in pretty good spirits most of the time; he even showed me how to take our bearings and taught me some of the other intricacies of navigation that were to stand me in good stead later. Occasionally he'd get to thinking about the fortune I'd dumped overboard and then he'd be pretty glum for a while, but what really griped him more than the loss of the swag was the fact that there had been twelve cartons of cigarettes in one of the suitcases I had jettisoned.

Between us we had had just thirty-two cigarettes when we took stock the morning of the second day, and Perry had been accustomed to smoking that many at least between suns. I enjoy a smoke pretty well myself occasionally, but I knew that I wouldn't suffer any without them; so I quit smoking entirely and saved my cigarettes for Perry, thinking that they might calm his nerves; and he cut himself down to three a day. For a while he seemed quite grateful to me for what he was pleased to call my sacrifice.

Each day I noticed that the ship seemed to be losing buoyancy; she lost altitude, but it was really not so serious as to cause me any alarm. Perry said that the consumption of oil, fuel, and food would compensate for any slight loss of gas that might be occurring. I took my turns at the controls; and during my hours off at night slept fitfully with one eye open, for I felt none too sure of Perry. And so the hours ran into days, and day followed day.

We saw nothing but the vast, sullen ocean rolling, rolling, rolling over the hidden mysteries of its gloomy depths; not a ship; not a sign of life. I came to hate the ocean, implacable, threatening; an insensate monster, boundless, merciless, always waiting, waiting, waiting for us down there below. I imagined that it knew that at last it would get us.

Perry had some books aboard; and I read a little, but my state of mind was such that I could not concentrate on what I was reading. I thought about my past life and tried not to think of the future. I thought a great deal about Daisy Juke. I recalled the disappointment I had felt when I had smelled liquor on her breath the last time that I had seen her. Of course I know that there are lots of perfectly respectable girls who take a drink occasionally, but it was something that our little crowd had never gone in for. It wasn't that we had any moral scruples against it; we just didn't do it. I remember in particular that Daisy used to say that inasmuch as the Lord hadn't given her any more brains than she needed it seemed silly to befuddle what she did have. Drink had caused a lot of suffering in her father's family, and she was very much opposed to it.

I wondered if Frank Adams had changed, too. He never wanted to be around with fellows who drank, because they bored and embarrassed him; and I had heard him say a dozen times that he would never marry a girl who drank. But perhaps he had changed; a great many of us do after we leave college and quite often without moral betterment.

And now Frank and Daisy were to marry! It hurt me a lot, for somehow I had never given up hope that someday – oh, what's the use? What chance could a dumb cop have had against Frank Adams? He had always beaten me out in everything worthwhile all our lives. I was never jealous of him nor ever bitter; I admired him too much, and he was my best friend. Whatever he won he deserved to win. But it sometimes seemed a little unfair that one fellow got everything and another nothing through no acquired virtue or fault of either, but just because the ancestors of one had happened to marry the right people and the ancestors of the other had not – just a matter of chromosomes. Chromosomes and the ocean! They are much alike; you can't change them, and you can't beat them.

It was early morning of the sixth day that the motor froze. We had considerable altitude, and it wouldn't be long until the sun warmed up the gas and checked our descent; so we were not particularly apprehensive. Perry went aft and commenced to tear the motor down to see what was wrong. There was room for only one man to work on it; so I couldn't help him any. I sat in the control room and looked down at the old devil rolling beneath us. We were settling toward those endless swells rolling on their senseless way incessantly just as they had for perhaps a billion years, just as they would for other billions of years, rolling over the bones of millions of men as they would roll over our bones . . . forever.

Hanging in the east, a hand span above the sea, the new sun was tempering the chill of the early morning air; already it was appreciably warmer, and with the rising temperature in the gas bag our rate of descent was lessening. Presently it would stop, or so I thought; but it didn't. We continued to drop very slowly.

The morning passed. Several times I walked back to see how Perry was getting along, but he was in no mood to be civil. Perry was one of those people who cannot be crossed and retain his equilibrium. When things were running smoothly, Perry's disposition was more or less tranquil; but when anything went wrong – blooey! – he went right up in the air and exploded like an aerial bomb.

He was that way now – the engine had crossed him; he said it had broken down to spite him, and he blamed me. Lots of otherwise sane people are illogical like that when things go wrong; only, Perry exaggerated it.

We were drifting along with a steady breeze about a hundred feet above the surface of the ocean, and we were still descending. I called his attention to our danger. He was leaning out of a small porthole at the stern which gave access to the motor, and at my words he drew himself back into the cabin and faced me. He held a heavy wrench in his hand. His features were contorted with rage, and there was that terrible light in his eyes.

He burst into a volley of profane abuse and came for me with the wrench. I stepped back and covered him with my gun. 'Cut it!' I snapped. 'And don't forget that now that the motor's gone haywire *I* don't need *you* any more.'

At that he lowered the wrench and stood there snarling at me. 'Now that you don't need me, I suppose you'll murder me. That's what I've been expecting right along; that's the best anyone could expect from scum like you.'

'Don't be a fool, Perry. Get busy and do something, or I

will. As long as you behave yourself, I won't interfere with the handling of the ship.'

'What do you want me to do?' he demanded. 'Haven't I been working all morning trying to make these repairs?'

'That's all right, but you ought to dump some water ballast now and get a little more altitude.' I had refrained from doing this myself because I had found that any independent action I took always aroused Perry's anger, and I didn't wish to irritate him; conditions were unpleasant enough at best.

'We don't have to dump any water ballast,' he snapped; 'that's for an emergency.'

'We are facing an emergency right now.'

'A college education did you a lot of good,' he sneered. 'Don't you know that heat will expand the gas in the bag? The sun will keep us up.'

I pointed through a window at the water billowing close beneath us. 'It isn't, though.'

'It's got to,' he insisted. 'I guess I know my physics.'

I turned toward the control room. 'Perhaps you do, Perry; but what we need now is altitude.'

'What you going to do?'

'Let out some water ballast.'

'If you do, I'll kill you!' he screamed, and at the same instant he hurled the wrench at my head.

I ducked, and it whizzed by my ear. I heard it crash into something behind me as Perry charged, his face a horrid mask of maniacal rage. I was glad that I didn't have to shoot him; it wasn't necessary now, for he was unarmed, and I have always been able to take care of myself where it was only a matter of fists and brawn.

He was sort of clawing at me as he rushed forward, as though he wanted to get hold of my jugular and tear it out, or, maybe, my heart. He was not a pretty picture. How different he looked from the Billy Perry I used to go to school with! It was as though another personality, both physical and spiritual, possessed him; and the change suggested, even in that moment of stress, the strange dual personality of that pathetic figure of Robert Louis Stevenson's imagination, Dr Jekyll.

Of course it didn't take as long for all this to happen as I am taking in the telling; he was on me the instant after the wrench flew by my head; but before his fingers closed upon my throat

I let him have a short jab to the chin. It wasn't a very hard blow (I didn't want to hit him as hard as I could; just enough to do the work), and he went down without another sound. He was out, all right.

Chapter Four

BATTLING A MANIAC

I LEFT Perry lying where he had fallen and went on into the control room, where I opened a valve and let the water run from the ballast tank. Presently we commenced to rise again, and I closed the valve; then I picked up the wrench he had thrown at me. As I did so, I saw what it had hit: the instrument board. The altimeter, compass, and oil gauge were wrecked. I tell you, things looked pretty hopeless to me right then. Not that I'd been harboring any great amount of hope before, but this seemed the last blow; for even if Perry were able to patch up the engine, the loss of the compass left us in a bad fix.

Perry was out for about ten minutes. When he came to, he got up and sat on the edge of his bunk looking sort of confused. 'What happened?' he asked.

'Oh, nothing,' I replied; 'you just tried to kill me, and I handed you the old K.O.'

'I don't remember,' he said. 'What was it all about?'

I told him, and he shook his head. He seemed dazed. 'Now listen to me, Perry,' I continued. 'This killing stuff has got to quit; if you make another break at me, I'm going to handcuff you. Furthermore, from now on I'll take charge; you'll do whatever I tell you. We're in a mess. I doubt if we ever get out of it. Anyway, throwing wrenches at me isn't going to help any.'

'I'm sorry,' he said. He appeared thoroughly cowed.

'Now, how about the engine?'

'It's gone, beyond repair.'

'So are the compass and the altimeter.'

'What happened to them?' he demanded. Again his manner changed; he showed excitement.

'When you threw the wrench at me it hit the instrument board.'

'It wouldn't have if you hadn't dodged,' he growled. He was slowly getting back to form. 'We're finished now; how can I navigate the ship without a compass?'

'You can do it as well now without a compass as with one; we haven't any engine,' I reminded him.

He didn't reply; just sat there on the edge of his cot staring at the floor. And there he sat all the rest of the day; not that it made any difference to me, for he wasn't the best of company anyway.

We gained altitude slowly all day up to about four o'clock. Of course, without the altimeter I could only guess at slight variations; but I should say that we didn't commence to drop appreciably until after five. After dark that night there was a light fog or haze lying close to the surface of the water, shutting it from our view. I sure missed the altimeter then.

About nine o'clock I told Perry to go into the control room and stand watch until midnight, after which I would relieve him until four in the morning. He got up without a word and went forward, and I stretched myself out on my cot. Sleeping in that little gondola with Perry at large was nerve-racking, but I hated to handcuff him until I was absolutely forced to do so. I know that I should have, but I didn't.

However, I slept so lightly that I heard his first footfall as he came from the control room into the cabin. 'Want anything?' I asked, sitting up.

'It's twelve o'clock,' he said.

So that was all it was! I realized that my nerves must be on edge if every time Perry moved I thought he was coming to kill me. Perhaps, however, under the circumstances, it is not so strange that I was that way; no one can imagine what the strain of those past six days had been.

I got up and went into the control room. Perry didn't lie down. He commenced pacing up and down the cabin. 'Better go to bed, Perry,' I suggested. 'You've had a hard day, and you ought to get some rest.'

He did not answer, but presently he commenced to mutter

to himself. I couldn't understand what he was saying. He kept up his pacing and his muttering, and I had to sit so that I could keep an eye on him.

I couldn't see anything from the windows of the control room. We were right in the fog now. Whether we were a thousand feet above the ocean or a hundred or ten there was no way of telling. To be on the safe side I opened the ballast tank valve again. By holding my hand on the valve handle I could feel the vibration caused by the water gurgling from the mouth of the pipe. It gave me a sense of relief for about a minute; then it stopped gurgling – the tank was empty!

For an hour I sat there hoping for the best and praying for daylight and the blessed rays of the sun. We were drifting with a gentle breeze, and I could see the fog wraiths twisting and curling in the diffused light from the cabin window. The fog appeared less dense now. Presently I saw something moving just below my eyes. It was the ocean! The fog was rolling but a few yards above the water, and we had dropped below it.

I sprang to my feet and ran back into the cabin where four five-gallon oil cans were stored. Hastily throwing open the gondola door, I started throwing the cans overboard.

Perry leaped from his cot. 'What are you doing?' he cried. 'Have you gone crazy?'

'We are almost in the ocean,' I explained, 'and the water ballast is all gone.'

'Don't throw that oil overboard, you fool!' he screamed.

I tossed another can through the doorway. 'Shut up! We don't need oil without an engine.'

He got up and came toward me. I thought I was in for another fight, but he said, 'All right; I'll help you.'

I picked up another can, and when I was near the doorway Perry threw himself upon my back and pushed me forward toward the opening. 'You be ballast, you lousy cop!' he yelled. 'That's all your damn carcass is good for.'

I dropped the can and lunged forward toward the open doorway, my arms outspread. I thought I was gone; but I managed to catch the frame with one hand, and though my body swung out I kept my handhold and my feet. Then he tried to push me out. He was laughing hysterically – a horrible laugh. He beat at my back and my head with one hand and pushed with the other. I could feel my fingers slipping from their hold. I couldn't think of anything to do, but I clung to life in grim desperation. I could see the ocean rolling silently a few feet below. It had been waiting for me all this time, and now it was going to get me. I wanted to curse it. Suddenly, in the reckless fury of hopelessness, I raised one foot from the floor and kicked back viciously. That foot was one of the frail props that were holding me poised on the brink of the grave; without its support I nearly pitched headlong into eternity. My heel caught Perry in the groin. He screamed with pain and fell back, and I managed to cling to my precarious hold and then scramble back into the cabin.

But Perry was not out; he was only hurt. He met me with a rush and we clinched. Then we went to the floor together. His one thought was to throw me overboard. I am larger and heavier and stronger than Perry. That is, ordinarily I am stronger; but he seemed now to be suddenly endowed with the strength of a dozen men. He was forcing me again toward the open doorway inch by inch. I tried to reach my gun, but couldn't; then I went for Perry's throat. He bit at me like a mad dog, but he never relinquished his efforts to push me into the ocean.

I spread my legs as far apart as I could and finally straddled the opening; that gave me a sense of greater security, but Perry kept on tugging and pulling and straining. It commenced to look as though the one who had the most endurance would be the victor. I couldn't notice that Perry was tiring in the least. I was still trying to reach his throat. At last I got a grip on his collar and pulled his head down toward me into a position that would expose his throat to my other hand.

Suddenly he opened his mouth and made a lunge at my jugular with his teeth. I jerked his head to one side, and he missed my throat but fastened his teeth in my shoulder. But then I got my fingers at his throat and commenced choking. He opened his jaws in a hurry; and as he raised his head to pull away from me, I got another hold with my free hand. Then, take my word for it, I choked. He was blue in the face and his tongue was lolling from his mouth when I dropped him.

I don't know why I didn't kill him then; I was certainly warranted in doing it. But I didn't relish the idea of killing men – not then. I got up and closed the door; then I sat down on the edge of my cot and tried to get my breath back. I was just about all in. Perry lay unconscious where I had left him. For a while I did not know but that I had killed him without meaning to, but no such luck.

Glancing through the open doorway, I saw that we were again enveloped in fog, and judged that the cans of oil I had thrown overboard had lightened us sufficiently to permit our again rising up into the fog layer; however, there was a chance that the fog might be lying on the surface of the water in places and, to be on the safe side, I threw over the remaining cans of oil.

Then I returned to Perry and, rolling him over on his back, slipped the bracelets around his wrists, securing his hands behind his back. He was commencing to show sings of reviving and was struggling and gasping like a fish out of water. Perhaps I should have felt sorry for him, but I am afraid that I didn't. His numerous vicious attacks on me had had their effect upon my nervous system, leaving me rather callous to his suffering.

The fight I had just been through, coupled with loss of sleep and nervous exhaustion over a period of days, left me pretty well done up; I was reasonably sure that the ship was rising from the immediate danger of foundering in the ocean and Perry was no longer a menace to my life, so I threw myself upon my cot and, despite Perry's struggles and groans, must have fallen asleep almost immediately.

I slept several hours, for it was daylight when I was awakened by a heavy body falling upon me; it was Perry. His wrists manacled behind him, he had launched himself upon me and was trying to reach my throat with his teeth. His face was distorted with rage and he was growling and frothing at the mouth. With my knees and hands I succeeded in pushing him off onto the floor, but as I leaped to my feet he was up and at me again.

I tried to keep him away from me without hurting him, but he followed me up, kicking and biting and butting with his head. He had become a raving maniac. Finally, I was compelled to knock him down; and this I had to do repeatedly, for the remnant of his mind seemed fixed by a single obsession that he must kill me.

Not once during this battle did he utter a word, but he made terrible noises that made every hair on my scalp feel as though it were standing on end. I have heard men and animals scream in rage and terror and death agonies, but I have never heard any sound as hideous as those that issued from Perry's foaming lips that morning in the fog above the Pacific.

I must have knocked him down half a dozen times before he finally lay still. It made me feel like a brute and a coward, this striking a man whose hands were fastened behind his back, but what else could I do? I had tried to get hold of him and pinion him down until I could truss him up in some way that would render him helpless; but he kicked and bit at me so viciously and, in his madness, had developed such tremendous strength that I was wholly unable to cope with him without risking terrible injuries myself.

After Perry went down for the count I hunted about for some rope to tie him with. While I was in the control room he regained consciousness and arose to his feet again. He stood there at the far end of the cabin with his head lowered, glaring at me.

'Perry,' I said, 'quiet down. I don't want to hurt you. Lie down and rest.'

He just stood there looking at me for a moment, his head weaving to and fro, sideways; then he turned and looked out of one of the windows into the fog. Suddenly he straightened up, his eyes lighted with a wild fire; it was as though he saw something out there in the fog. 'Mother!' he screamed. 'Mother! I am coming!' And then, before I could interfere, he took a couple of quick steps and dove headforemost through the glass of the window and disappeared among the writhing mist wraiths that enveloped us.

Chapter Five

DERELICT OF THE AIR

I WAS ALONE. Perhaps no one was ever more utterly alone than I. Far out over the Pacific, without knowledge of my exact location, the sole occupant of a tiny dirigible drifting at the mercy of the elements in the midst of a dense fog, I felt as utterly and permanently detached from the rest of the world and from humanity as though I had been transported to the inhospitable surface of the dead moon. And perhaps the most depressing feature of my situation was its complete hopelessness. I am not an imaginative man, and I could now conceive no circumstance through which escape from my predicament might be reasonably expected to develop.

For six days we had been sailing above the ocean; we had covered between five and six thousand miles as closely as I could compute it, and we had not seen a single sail by day nor light by night nor even the faint smudge of a distant steamer's smoke beyond the horizon. I had come to feel as though all other life had been wiped from the face of the earth.

However, there are lots worse things than being alone: having Perry as a companion, for instance. I was glad Perry had gone. It was far better so. One can scarcely imagine the sense of relief I felt now that the terrible incubus of constant apprehension was removed. And as though Nature joined me in joyous celebration of my release, the fog dissolved and the sun enveloped me in the warmth of its welcome embrace.

I felt almost happy – at least a certain contentment of resignation – for I was physically comfortable; I had food, water, a place to sleep, and for the time being, at least, I was warm.

For the future? Well, I have never been particularly fearful of death; and perhaps at this time I was more indifferent to life than ordinarily. I do not mean by this that I wanted to die or that I would not have exerted every effort to live; I am merely trying to convey the truth, that the outcome did not seem to interest me greatly. And there were two factors that contributed practically all of this mental attitude: one was a vast curiosity that I had always entertained concerning the mysteries of the life beyond; the other was the knowledge that I had definitely and for all time lost Daisy Juke.

My love for her had always seemed so hopeless that I do not know why the definite announcement of her coming marriage should have affected me as it did; but then, Hope is a rather peculiar animal. Fed upon nothing, he thrives; set upon, beaten, murdered, he refuses to die. Even though I knew that Hope was dead in my bosom, I suppose that I still hoped to have Daisy some day, notwithstanding the fact that I knew I should never survive the adventure upon which chance had embarked me.

Lightened from the weight of Perry's body, the dirigible quickly gained altitude; and as her gas was warmed by the sun, she rose still higher. A brisk wind had arisen, and we were drifting rapidly toward the southwest. As usual, when the weather was clear, I was scanning the surface of the ocean for a ship. Really, I don't know what I should have done about it if I had seen a ship; I couldn't maneuver the dirigible without an engine, and a ship anywhere, except directly beneath me, would have been more of an aggravation than a blessing.

Of course, the ship might sight me and change her direction for the purpose of investigating so remarkable a phenomenon as a dirigible in mid-Pacific; but I really didn't have much hope of that.

There was a parachute aboard, and if a ship sighted me and approached, it was my intention to jump and take a chance on being picked up by a small boat. But these were only day-dreams, for there was no ship in sight. I had commenced to believe that there were no ships on the Pacific.

That night we lost altitude rapidly after dark, and to make matters worse the wind increased until it was blowing a gale. As I think I have mentioned before, the dirigible was of frail construction. The gondola was not an integral part of the frame, but was suspended a few feet below the gas bag by ropes, much as the basket of a balloon is attached. It all seemed very flimsy in fair weather; and now, with a gale blowing and an angry sea rising close below, I felt that nothing short of a miracle could prevent utter disaster.

Nevertheless, I was determined not to give up without a fight; and so I went to work throwing out the less-useful articles that I could spare first. But these were so few and their combined weight so little that the result was only to check the speed of our descent and not stop it.

Whipped by the gale, which was constantly increasing in violence, the gondola bucked like a bronco. Several times I was thrown violently to the floor and once almost hurled through the window out of which Perry had dived. Heavy clouds obscured the moon and the stars, yet there was sufficient luminosity to reveal the angry waves breaking below; and the sight of them there so close spurred me to action.

I thought of the engine, a now useless encumbrance; and finding a wrench, I made my way aft to the little porthole which gave access to it. As I leaned far out in the darkness, there was a vivid flash of lightning that revealed the proximity of the raging waters; and this was followed by peal after peal of deafening thunder – a wholly unnecessary waste of Nature's energy, for I was already as terrified as I well could be and retain control of my faculties.

The engine was supported by a metal frame that was bolted in four places to the frame of the gondola. The two upper nuts were within easy reach, but the lower ones were so far beneath the opening through which I leaned that almost my entire body was hanging out of the porthole before I could reach them with my hand.

Almost immediately after the first flash of lightning rain commenced to fall in torrents. I could feel it beating the dirigible lower and lower, pressing it down with the weight of a million tiny hands. The gondola was whipping this way and that. Momentarily, I expected to be pitched headlong into the sea.

At last I got a bite on one of the lower nuts with the wrench. It was a large, heavy nut screwed firmly down upon a lock washer. Even under favorable conditions it would have been hard to start; now it appeared hopeless. But one never knows to what heights of achievement he may rise until Death has him by the tail with a downhill pull.

I threw every ounce of my strength and all the weight that I dared into a supreme effort – and the nut started. After that it was easy, as far as that nut was concerned. The wind and the rain were cold, but by the time that nut dropped into the ocean I was wringing wet with perspiration as well as rain-water.

The second of the lower nuts gave me a terrible battle; it seemed to have been turned home even more firmly than its fellow. Then, even after I got it started and turned part way off, another obstacle presented itself: the threads near the end of the bolt had been jammed! And now the ocean was perilously close beneath; some of the mightier waves rose almost to the gondola.

To turn off the nut over the jammed threads was a slow and arduous job, and always the ocean was reaching its cold claws up to drag me down. There are a lot of people who love the ocean; I used to think that I did, but I don't try to fool myself anymore – I hate it. It is beautiful in its own sinister way in many of its moods; but is like a cold, hard woman of the under world, whose hands are stained with the blood of many men, who, like the ocean, has murdered her lovers.

When the second nut fell I was almost exhausted, but I might not even pause to catch my breath. Immediately I fell to work upon one of the upper nuts. A great wave rose far above any that had preceded it, and at the same moment some vagary of the storm forced the dirigible suddenly a little lower. I felt the gale-swept spindrift driving against my cheek, and the next instant the crest of a wave slapped resoundingly against the bottom of the dirigible.

Death seemed very close. I could feel his cold hands in the chill of the unpreaching waves. The voice of the gale was the howling of his ghostly retinue. That time Death had missed me by a few feet; but next time he might not, for once we dropped low enough to permit a single wave to break above the sills of the gondola's windows we should never rise again; and each succeeding wave would drag us deeper.

I knew that getting nervous and excited would not help matters any, and so I worked as calmly and coolly as I would have had no emergency existed. I must admit that it took a lot of willpower to do it and that inwardly I was frantic. Some malign force seemed to prevent those nuts from starting until I felt that further effort was useless; then they would give a little, grudgingly. Afterward, the slow process of turning the nut off the bolt, the rain, the wind, the thunder, and the lightning all combining with the bucking of the gondola to tear the wrench from my cold-numbed fingers, almost jolted my mind loose from its foundations.

But at last the third nut dropped into the sea. Only one was left. As I worked on it another wave struck the gondola, this time higher up. A little wave dashed through the broken window. Another of those big fellows would swamp us.

The engine frame was still hanging on the protruding bolts, and I was commencing to fear that I might have difficulty in prying it off after I got the fourth nut removed. This one had started more easily than the others, and I was laboriously turning it off when a mountainous wave struck the gondola a terrific blow. The frail ship staggered and reeled, and as it did so the engine frame slipped from the heads of the three bolts from which I had removed the nuts; the gondola shipped water, and its stern dropped into the trough behind the sea that had struck it. The engine swung free; and its weight, combined with the sudden, twisting jerk of the gondola, snapped the remaining bolt.

As the engine disappeared beneath the waves, the stern of the gondola rose above the next comber; a moment later a flash of lightning showed me that the ship was rising. I drew my body back through the porthole and sat down on the floor of the cabin, my back against a wall. I was exhausted. An inch or so of water was sloshing back and forth the length of the cabin as the ship careened wildly in the gale; but it could not add any to my discomfort, for I was already wet to the skin.

That night! All of its horrors are engraved indelibly upon my memory. The wind increased; I think it must have approached the violence of a hurricane. The ship was tossed and whirled about like a feather; every instant I expected that it would be torn to pieces. How it withstood the buffeting of the storm is beyond me.

When morning came, I saw that we were but a few hundred feet above the water; the chill air and the weight of the rain-soaked envelope of the gas bag were holding us down. The night had been spent in darkness, the batteries that lighted the cabin having suddenly ceased to function. Whether it was because the generation that had charged them had gone out of commission with the engine, or the sea water had flooded them and caused a short circuit in the wiring system, I did not know; but I did know that the batteries dead were of more value to me than before; they represented weight that I could throw overboard.

They would have gone before the engine had I known where they were located. As soon as it was light enough, I commenced to search for them. Eventually I found them in a box beneath the cabin floor, and when they had gone after the engine and I had managed to drain the sea water from the cabin we gained altitude steadily.

Shortly after dawn the rain stopped, but the wind still howled about me like a demon gone mad. At that, however, it proved helpful; it dried the cordage and the envelope and so relieved the dirigible of weight that it continued to rise steadily until we must have had several thousand feet of altitude by noon.

For three days the wind blew violently, and little by little I stripped the gondola of everything I could pry loose to throw overboard. When we dropped closer to the ocean I could see that the seas were enormous. It was under such conditions that I sighted a ship.

We must have been drifting about a thousand feet above the surface. I had been sitting on the edge of my bunk eating. It was not often now that I took the trouble to look down at the ocean; the less I saw of it the better I was suited. But when I got up after eating, I chanced to look through one of the windows; and there was a ship right in the path of our drifting and only a short distance ahead.

It was a big freighter, and it certainly looked good to me. It was the only thing I had seen in a week to assure me that I was not the sole inhabitant of a world.

I thought it must be heavily laden, for even at the altitude I was, I could see that it was riding low in the water; every now and then a big sea broke over it. I must have been a little mad even to contemplate jumping, but I could see nothing but death awaiting me if I stuck to the dirigible; and that ship looked so good to me, so big and safe, that I couldn't imagine but that its captain would find a way to pick me up. If luck were with me, I might even manage to alight on the ship's deck. What madness! I realize it now; but then, after what I had passed through, I was willing to risk the chance of death just to escape from that derelict flying coffin that I felt was carrying me surely to my grave.

Hastily I donned the parachute that Perry had brought along for himself in the event that he was compelled to bail out; then I pushed the gondola door open. The dirigible was pitching about crazily, and I had to cling tightly to the sides of the doorway to keep from being thrown out.

The wind was carrying us steadily toward the position of the freighter. I wanted to time my jump so that after the chute opened the wind would continue to carry me toward the vessel and not beyond it; therefore, I planned to jump before we were over it.

It was a rather difficult problem to figure, and I realized that it was only guesswork at the best; but at last the time came. Perhaps I should have breathed a prayer, but I didn't. From some reason I took a deep breath, looked down at the great freighter wallowing in the seas below, and then –

Chapter Six

INTO THE SEA

I BREAK into a cold sweat even now when I think how close I came to jumping. My salvation was just a matter of a split second. I was poised to throw myself out; I had even loosened my hold on the door frame, and was thinking about the rip cord on the chute and hoping the latter would function properly, when an enormous sea broke over the bow of the freighter. For a moment the entire ship was obliterated by a foaming maelstrom of water; then the stern rose high above the waves until it stood almost vertical. It poised there for a few seconds; then it slid swiftly beneath the waves. The great freighter was no more.

For a moment I stood there horrified, looking down at the empty sea; then I hastily closed the door, removed the parachute, and threw myself on my bunk. I don't mind admitting that hope was pretty nearly at low ebb right then.

Toward the end of the third day the storm had abated, the sky was clear, the sun was hot; but even so, the bag had lost so much buoyancy that I feared the ship could not keep the air during a long, cold night. By this time I had jettisoned everything that I could spare. Water and food I would not sacrifice; and I kept my clothing, my gun, and my ammunition. I had hated to throw the books overboard, but they had gone the night before – every ounce counted.

I had kept some tools: a knife, a hand ax, and a light crowbar. I had had a purpose in keeping these, and now I felt that the time was approaching when I should find use for them. Nearly everything had gone overboard to reduce the load; there remained nothing but the gondola.

The floor of the cabin was of very light planking; and with the aid of the hand ax and the crowbar I commenced ripping this up, leaving a couple of planks down the center as a walkway. From some of the others I constructed a light affair about eighteen inches wide and six feet long. It was not a work of art. Lacking a saw, I had been compelled to hack pieces to approximately proper lengths with the hand ax. The planks were held together by four battens secured by nails I had salvaged from the flooring. Most of these nails were bent and had to be straightened. With my crude tools, the entire job was a slow one; but at last it was complated.

As I worked I saw that we were losing altitude again, and from time to time I pitched over a plank or two. This always helped for a time, but as the sun dropped lower and the air grew cooler our rate of descent became more pronounced; then I pitched overboard all the remaining lumber except the little platform I had built. Immediately, we went soaring up into the air; and inevitably my spirits rose, as they always did with a rise in altitude. But I still feared for the outcome of the long night ahead.

With that thought spurring me on, I went ahead with the work I had commenced. With my knife I cut a strip eighteen inches wide from the mattress on my cot, throwing the balance overboard. This strip I lashed to my little platform.

Now I set to work upon the ceiling of the gondola with my hand ax, chopping at the framework until I had cut a hole in the forward part large enough to permit my body to pass through. Taking a couple of half-hitches around one end of the platform, I fastened the other end of the rope about my waist and clambered through the hole I had made out onto the roof of the gondola.

About four feet above my head billowed the envelope of the gas bag, no longer taut and bulging with gas as upon the day we had taken off but loose and flabby like the neck of an old woman who needs face-lifting. It was evident that we had lost a considerable amount of the element that stood between me and a watery grave, if you will pardon the lack of congruity.

The rope I had attached to the platform was part of a hundred foot coil that Perry had brought along smong a heterogeneous stock of supplies. One end was fastened about my waist, and I drew up a few more feet and secured a loop of it to one of the cables with which the gondola was attached to the gas bag. This was a precaution against the possibility of an accident pitching me overboard.

Next I drew the platform to the roof of the gondola and made it fast, temporarily, so that some misadventure might not rob me of the fruits of my labor.

This done, I attached the ends of four pieces that I cut from the coil of rope in such a way that four loops depended about four feet below the gas bag, there being a little less than two feet distance between loops. Through these loops I pushed the platform, adjusting its position until it hung level beneath the gas bag; then I lashed the loops securely to the platform in the eight places that they touched its sides. My next job was to run a handline along each side of the platform about two feet above it.

I now had about twenty feet of rope left; and with this, after making several trips down into the cabin to fetch them, I slung my supplies of water and food in such a way that they would hang beneath the platform, yet easily accessible to my reach. I also brought up my blankets, folded them to the proper width, and lashed them on top of my mattress. The parachute I fastened in a position at one end of the platform so that I could use it as a pillow if I wished. I also fastened my own life line securely to one of the guy ropes.

Darkness had fallen long before I completed my task, but a full moon had given me ample light by which to see. I still had an altitude of several hundred feet, the sea was calm, a gentle wind was bearing me west-southwest. For the moment at least I had nothing to worry about and could relax. Under these conditions, and with the appetite of a farm hand, I ate a meal that would scarcely have satisfied a canary bird; for even though I doubted that the bag could stay afloat as long as my food might be made to last, I was taking no chances on adding starvation to my other woes.

Having eaten, I crawled beneath the blankets on my narrow couch and was soon asleep, my last conscious thought a hope that the ship would stay in the air throughout the night.

I must have slept soundly throughout nearly the entire night, for when a little jar and an accompanying splash awoke me the stars had faded from the eastern sky. With returning consciousness I was aware of a new sensation of motion: a gentle upward sweep followed by a drop accompanied by such a splashing sound as had awakened me.

The sight that met my sleepy gaze brought me to instant and full wakefulness: the gondola was afloat. I recall how thankful I was that this had not happened during the height of the storm, the only reminders of which now were the long swells rolling endlessly. How cold and relentless the ocean looked! I thought of the poor devils who had gone down with the freighter, and wondered how long it would be before I joined them.

However, my position was neither surprising nor shocking. I had been expecting it. In a way I had been awaiting it. My labors of the previous afternoon had been in anticipation of this very eventuality. They had been in preparation for the casting off of the useless weight of the gondola, which I had feared to attempt while in the air lest the severing of the next to final rope and the sudden surge of all the gondola's weight as it swung downward might rip the gas bag open.

Now the car was temporarily floating on the surface of the sea; there would be no sudden strains exerted as I severed the ropes that held it to the gas bag. My only danger lay in the possibility that the gondola might fill with water and sink before I had succeeded in cutting it loose.

Spurred on by this far from remote contingency, I lost no time in falling to work with my knife upon the numerous cables that ran from the envelope of the gas bag to the gondola. But I soon discovered that my knife was a wholly inadequate tool for this purpose; the cables were heavy, and the knife soon dulled.

The gondola was slowly filling and already settling steadily; it would have been entirely submerged before I could have cut half the cables with my knife.

I had intended cutting most of them the evening before, while still in the air; but I had been very tired and had taken a chance on the ship remaining out of water until after I had snatched a little sleep. I had not expected to sleep all night; I had never done so before.

Abandoning the knife, I fell to work on the cables with the hand ax; and when I say I fell to work that doesn't begin to convey a picture of my activity during the following few minutes. The cables parted easily to lusty blows from the sharp edge of the ax. The gondola was settling lower and lower. There were two more strands of cable, both amidships on opposite sides of my platform.

I severed one and the gas bag tilted as the freed side rose. The platform on which I stood tipped at a perilous angle. I clung desperately to one of the supporting ropes and swung a vicious cut at the remaining cable – and missed it.

Just then a big roller swept against the gondola and poured through the open windows; the next instant the water swept about my knees, so quickly did the gondola sink as it filled with water. I made another pass at the cable, and this time I struck it squarely with the center of the ax blade. I think that blow would have cut through a half inch bar of iron; it was certainly full of enthusiasm and ginger. It severed the remaining cable, but there was still an instant of suspense. The platform was now fully a foot under water. The gas bag seemed to be tugging to drag it upward, the ocean to drag it down. Which would win? I was much interested in the answer.

I was standing in the center of the platform which was almost horizontal. Like the drowning man that I was, I grasped for the only straw in sight, and ran quickly to one end of the platform. That end sank until I was submerged to the waist, but the other end rose out of the water. Now, the pressure of the water on the submerged end, instead of retarding the upward pull of the gas bag on the elevated end, accelerated it; and a moment later I was surging upward at an astonishing rate, far above the ocean. What a relief it was for me, as well as the gas bag, to get rid of that gondola.

As I rose swiftly into the new morning, the sun came up out of the eastern ocean; and once again my hopes rose. I was soaking wet to the waist, but I was almost happy. I would celebrate with another canary meal. It was then that a dark cloud obliterated the rising sun of my new hope. My food supply had been reduced to Swedish bread, chocolate, crackers, and jerky. I had suspended it in a canvas sack beneath the platform, and the platform had been a foot or so under water.

Fearfully, I drew the sack up onto the platform, opened it, and looked in. What a mess! Crackers, chocolate, jerky, bread, and the pulp of cardboard cartons soaked together with sea water in a sickly coglomerate. My heart sank. I thought I would swear; but as there was no one to hear me it didn't seem worth the effort. It is remarkable how many of our reactions are dependent upon an audience.

I picked out a few pieces of jerky, cleaned them off the best I could, and ate them. The natural taste of jerky is such that there is little might befall it that would make it any worse, but I found that it increased my thirst. That was unfortunate, as my water supply was all too limited.

Having eaten and drunk, without pleasure and apparently without profit, I removed my wet clothing and hung it where the wind and sun would dry it. Far below lay the sea, and it was evident that what had started out in life as a dirigible and was now a free balloon was still rising. Presently I commenced to feel cold; and as my clothing had dried rapidly, I donned it.

Still we rose; and the farther up we went the colder I got, notwithstanding the fact that the sun was shining brightly. After a while I had to crawl between my blankets. That night I thought I was going to freeze to death. I was never so cold in my life, but the next night I was colder. Even the lower temperatures failed to bring the balloon down to warmer altitudes.

Two days and two nights of this left me almost hopeless, though why I should previously have entertained any hopes I do not know. I spent that second night trying to decide whether I should die a slow death of cold, starvation, and thirst in the air or dive overboard without my parachute. I had reached no decision when the sun rose; so I remained shivering between my blankets, too cold and miserable to even put myself out of my misery.

After a while I thought that I would look over the edge of my magic carpet to see how much of a dive it would be if I finally determined to do the sensible thing. Like a snail from its shell, I wriggled a little way out of my blankets and looked down.

My heart almost stopped. Just beneath me was a large island! I could see other islands dotting the sea ahead. Hastily I threw the blankets aside; then I took another look. That island was a long way down. I unlashed the parachute from the platform and strapped it to my body. Then I took another look. I had never made a parachute leap. The prospect appalled me; I seemed to have forgotten that a moment before I had been contemplating jumping without a parachute. I wondered if I would hit the island or fall into the sea. I knew that if I waited too long I should drift past the island. Grasping the ring of the rip cord firmly, I jumped.

I fell about ten feet and was stopped with a sudden jerk. I had forgotten to cast off my life line, one end of which was secured about my body, the other end to the rigging above the platform.

Luckily I had not pulled the rip cord; but even so, my predicament was a most unhappy one. As I dangled there, apparently helpless, I knew that the wind was surely carrying the balloon across the island and that presently we should be over the sea again.

Chapter Seven

THE VULTURE

I DO NOT KNOW how high up I was; I can only guess. That guess would be somewhere between five thousand and ten thousand feet. I know the ground seemed a rather terrifying distance away. Hanging on the end of that rope with nothing solid to rest my feet on was an appalling experience.

I had been no safer on the frail platform swinging beneath the gas bag, but I had felt safer. It is just one of those things that are so hard to explain. In such instances intellect is swept into the background, and we react to primordial urges whose roots lie in a time before man existed.

Now that I looked down I wondered that I had ever been silly enough to leap from the security of my little platform into that abyss bottomed by death. I tried to climb up my life line and regain the platform; but the cumbersome straps and buckles of the parachute, and its weight, so hindered me that I was forced to give up the idea.

Then, gradually, sanity returned. I mastered my shaken nerves. I try not to think of what I passed through during those brief moments after I had leaped from the platform. Of course it is natural that a man should try to find excuses for his faults. For a long time after the event I argued with myself that I was weakened by hunger, exposure, fatigue, and the long days and nights of nervous strain that I had undergone since I had leaped aboard the dirigible nearly two weeks before, that I was not myself, not responsible. But the fact remains, regardless of extenuations, I was in a blue funk.

Fortunately for me I managed to come out of it just in time; and reaching into one of my pockets, I withdrew my knife and cut the life line.

As I hurtled downward I pulled the rip cord, and when a sudden jerk assured me that the chute had opened I breathed the first sigh of real relief that I had experienced in almost two weeks. Gad! How glad I was to leave that crazy invention of the mad Perry.

From the altitude of the balloon I had been unable to recognize objects on the island; it had been merely a flat blob of green on a blue ocean, a broken border of pale yellow and white was the sand and surf.

As I dropped lower the island became larger. I saw that there was little likelihood that I should miss it, though the wind was carrying me slowly toward its western extremity. Hills and valleys took shape; the green became trees and shrubs and grasses. A speck just off the western shore developed into a vessel, and then some specks that had not been there before appeared upon the widening beach.

These specks were moving about. Presently, I determined that they were men. They seemed to be acting very strangely. Now I saw little puffs of smoke apparently rising from them at irregular intervals; and later, if any doubts had remained in my mind as to what these puffs signified, I heard the reports of firearms.

Now I knew that the enlarging specks were men, men occupied in the age-old activity of men, the business of killing other men. I knew now that they were not lions or tigers or hyenas just from the fact that they were killing one another, if from nothing else.

As I floated downward it became more and more apparent that I was going to alight either on the beach among these men or in the water very close to shore. In either event I should be discovered by them. I could see them quite distinctly now, and it was evident that they had not yet seen me.

They appeared to be brown men. Several of them were naked to the waist. Some had colored cloths wound about their heads. Two or three wore only loin cloths. They were fighting with muskets, pistols, and curved swords. A small boat was drawn up on the beach just out of reach of the surf.

From the positions of the two factions engaged in the discussion I assumed that one of them had landed in this boat from the small vessel lying a short distance offshore in a little bay; the other was defending a pathway that led up a low cliff at the upper end of the beach.

The defending party had evidently made a sortie shortly before; now they were being driven back or, rather, they were making strenuous efforts to get back before they were annihilated.

Just before I alighted I was discovered. There was a great deal of excited shouting and gesticulation. Everyone stopped fighting and stared at me. As luck would have it, I came down between the opposing factions, and for a moment both sides just stood there staring at me. Which was fortunate for me, since it gave me time to free myself from the parachute harness.

As I did so, a big black near whom I had alighted, and who evidently belonged to the crew of the small boat, came at me with a cutlass. I whipped my gun from its holster and shot him in the belly. Thus my allegiance was determined.

The defenders raised a whoop of savage appreciation and launched a new sortie. One of the invaders aimed a musket at me; but before he could pull the trigger, I shot him between the eyes. After that, the enemy retreated.

A big, bearded fellow, the only white man among them, was shouting orders in a tongue strange to me; that is, mostly strange. It was interlarded with familiar English oaths. He and several of his fellows ran to launch the small boat, while the others held us off. This was not difficult, because the defenders seemed only too glad to see the others departing.

I had fired only in self-defense. The fight was none of my business; I didn't even know what it was about, nor who in the right nor who in the wrong. Therefore I took no more part in the affair, but watched my howling allies as they shrieked and cursed at the departing foe.

There were several dead and wounded men lying about on the beach. The fellow I had shot in the belly was groaning in agony. Another wounded man was lying near me; he was a white man, a sallow-complexioned fellow with a thin, cruel mouth. Two men were standing over him, watching him. The groaning of the Negro evidently annoyed him for he spoke sharply to one of the men, at the same time nodding toward the black; and the fellow he had spoken to walked over and ran his cutlass through the Negro's heart. It was the most cold-blooded thing I had ever seen done up to that time; yet, in a way, it was merciful, too. The man couldn't have lived.

Now, the man who had ordered the killing turned his eyes on me; and as I glanced about I saw that several others were watching me, too. They were a mean-looking lot, and their glances were none too friendly.

My uniform, after what it had been through, was a sorry looking mess; yet it was a uniform all right. You know what some of those motorcycle cop uniforms are like; a British field marshal's has nothing on them. The Glenora uniform was a work of art.

Just looking at those fellows about me was enough to convince anyone that they were not the sort who would welcome a field marshal of any nationality with open arms.

'Who are you?' asked the wounded white man. He addressed me in Spanish, which I understand well, having studied it for four years in high school and college in addition to using it whenever an opportunity presented itself during my contacts with Mexicans, who are numerous in southern California. Languages came easily to me, and in addition to Spanish I had a good working knowledge of French. I was to find that my mastery of both of these languages was to stand me in good stead in the days to come.

'I am an American,' I replied. 'My name is Lafitte.'

'What are you doing here?'

'I was blown to sea in a dirigible. This is the first land I have seen in two weeks; I had no food and little water. Naturally, I bailed out.' I looked up and then pointed. 'There is what remains of my ship.'

Every eye followed the direction indicated by my index finger. It took most of them a long time to locate the little speck far up and to the west.

'How is it that you speak Spanish?' he asked. 'You say that you are an American.' There was a note of suspicion in his voice.

I explained, after which he held a whispered conference with the two men nearest him. I caught snatches of their conversation, but it was in a language I could not understand. The two appeared to be urging some action which he was not wholly in accord; they often gesticulated angrily in my direction, shooting dark glances at me that were far from friendly; but the white man demurred.

Finally he spoke sharply in a tone that silenced them; then they lifted him between them, and at the same time he spoke to me. 'You will come with us,' he said. 'I want to talk to you further before I decide what to do with you.'

I followed them up the narrow trail to the summit of the cliff, where the trail entered a dense growth of trees and underbrush. Behind me came three ornery-looking customers with muskets and cutlasses. From the expressions upon their faces it appeared that they would have liked to use them on me.

Two or three hundred yards from the cliff we came to a clearing several acres in extent, in the center of which was a building designed after the manner of an old Spanish ranch house. It was rectangular in shape, one-storied, and built around a large central patio. Several very small windows pierced the outside walls which were otherwise blank.

My first impression was that the place had been designed to withstand assault, nor did more intimate knowledge of the building and its master tend to destroy this first impression. The walls were thick, the single pair of gates through which we entered the patio were massive, and the small windows well adapted to the uses of defending riflemen. But what was the need of such a fortress on this tiny island?

At the gate were a few armed ruffians similar to those who accompanied us, and in the shade of covered porches within the patio I saw a number of young women. Lying in the shade or wandering about the patio were dogs, pigs, and chickens.

At one end of the patio was a low wall pierced by a single gate through which I followed the Spaniard and the two men who were supporting him into a smaller patio, which I learned later was reserved for the master, and on which his living quarters opened. The other men did not follow us into this enclosure.

A white girl who was lying in a hammock in the shade of a porch raised herself on one elbow and survyed us as we entered. Her face was beautiful, her expression sullen.

'What is the matter with you?' she demanded of the Spaniard.

'We had a little brush with the Portuguese; one of his men nearly got me.'

'Too bad he didn't.' She spoke a strange mixture of French and Spanish.

The Spaniard's lip curled in a smile that was half snarl. 'When I die, you die; don't forget that, you little devil. I have given orders.'

She shrugged; then she let her gaze rest on me. 'Who is that, a prisoner?'

The Spaniard did not reply; and a moment later his men had helped him across the porch and into the house, where they laid him on a bed. I stopped just inside the doorway. He nodded to me to come nearer.

'You don't happen to be a doctor, do you?' he asked.

I shook my head.

'Know anything at all about the care of a wound?'

'A little, of course.'

'Well, you'd be better than these damn natives. Have a

look at it, and see what you can do. These fellows will see that you have anything you need that we happen to have, which, of course, isn't much.'

'Have you any antiseptics?' I asked.

'No.'

His shirt and breeches were soaked with blood. With the help of the two men, I undressed him; and at my suggestion he sent one of the men to boil water and cloths for washing and bandaging the wound. An examination revealed that the slug had entered his right side and come out of his back near the spine. One rib was shattered, but apparently neither the lung nor spine had been touched. However, it was an ugly wound.

When the water and cloths had been prepared, I cleaned up those two holes the best I could and bandaged him up. He was a nervy fellow. He must have been suffering terribly, but he never let out a whimper. When he spoke, his tone was quite as casual as though nothing unusual were affecting him. He sent one of the men for brandy, and when it was brought he asked me to join him in a drink. He emptied a tumblerful without lowering the glass from his lips. I took one swallow of the stuff; it was like drinking fire, but it certainly bucked me up. I hadn't eaten anything but a little dilapidated jerky in two days, and that fiery liquid on an empty stomach had a most remarkable effect. I felt as though I owned the island; another drink, and I could have gone out and licked an army. But I had sense enough not to take another drink.

How the Spaniard could have drunk the quantity he did and remained either conscious or coherent was beyond me, but the only effect it had was to brace him up a little.

'Do you know who I am?' he asked.

I told him that I did not.

'Do you know the name of this island?'

'I do not even know in what part of the world I am. For nearly two weeks I have been blown around in a disabled airship without a compass.'

He was studying my uniform. 'Are you an army officer?' he demanded.

'I am a motorcycle policeman.'

'And you are an American,' he mused. 'You couldn't have been looking for me.'

'Certainly not. I was not looking for anyone, and I do not even know who you are.'

'I am the Vulture,' he said, and he eyed me narrowly.

The name meant nothing to me, and if he were expecting any reaction from his announcement he was disappointed.

'The Vulture,' he repeated, as though he thought that perhaps I had not heard aright the first time.

'Well, what of it?' demanded the brandy I had drunk.

He seemed to be taken aback both by my reply and my tone. He scowled. 'You mean that you have never heard of the Vulture?' he demanded.

'Never,' he replied.

He thought for a moment, and then he nodded understandingly. 'Of course America is a long way from here, and it is possible that there are Americans who never have heard of me,' he admitted.

'Well, just who are you?' I asked.

He thought a moment before he replied; then he shrugged. 'It will do no harm to tell you. No one who comes to this island leaves it alive, except as he serves in my company; so whatever knowledge you gain you cannot use against me.'

'I have no reason for harming you,' I replied, and I certainly don't want to remain forever on this island. I want to get back to America.'

'You will never return to America. I have not decided what I shall do with you. I may kill you, or I may not; but you may rest assured that you will never see America again.' He spoke with the finality of one who is accustomed to ordering the lives of those about him.

'That is interesting,' I commented.

'Perhaps,' he admitted. 'But to get back to the subject. My profession is of such a nature that it would be disastrous were word of it or my whereabouts to be carried to any of the nations that have possessions or mandates in this part of the world, and they are many – Dutch, British, French, American.

'To the authorities I am little more than a name and a fable, a part of the folklore of Malaysia. That is because when I strike there is no one left to carry news of me to my enemies. There are just vague, whispered rumors concerning me; and there would not be even those had I been more careful when I first set out upon this business of mine. Then, I used to be careless of the men that were associated with me; and some of them talked too much when they went to Singapore or Saigon or Batavia. But now I have men who do not talk too much, even when they drink too much.

'A pearler disappears. Perhaps it was wrecked; no one knows. It never comes to any port, and only the Vulture knows why. But I am that much richer, and I do not have to risk my life diving for pearls. Sometimes other vessels disappear; they are usually small vessels, but their cargoes are always rich.

'We live well; my men are contented. We divide the profits, half to them and half to me. Once a year we spend a month or two in Singapore or, perhaps, Manila. That is our vacation. It is well for businessmen to enjoy a vacation at least once a year.'

So! My friend, the Vulture, was a pirate. I should have been shocked. My parents are God-fearing, law-abiding people; training, education, environment, all my past experiences, all my ambitions for the future should have rendered piracy a loathsome thing to me. Yes, most assuredly I should have been shocked; but I was not. I felt a strange thrill as I contemplated the Vulture and his life. There seemed a bond between us drawing me toward him and his calling. It was no bond of loyalty nor affection. I cannot explain it. I neither liked nor disliked the man. I could have as easily bared a cutlass and given my life in his defense or cut his throat with it. No, I cannot explain it, except, possibly, upon the hypothesis of a pirate psychology that had come down to me from old Jean Lafitte, the French corsair of the Gulf of Mexico.

Chapter Eight

LA DIABLESA

THE VULTURE FINISHED a quart bottle of rum and said that he felt better. 'I think I can sleep now,' he announced. 'Call *La Diablesa*.'

'The young lady on the porch?' I inquired at a venture.

'*Sí*, and hurry; I am very sleepy.'

I stepped to the doorway. The girl was still lying in the hammock. '*Señorita*,' I called, 'he wishes to speak to you,' and I nodded toward the wounded man.

She arose languidly and came toward me. There was an undulating eccentric hip movement in her walk. Her figure was divine. The combination may best be described as, body by Fisher, bearings by Timkin. I stepped aside as she entered the room. Her body exhaled the fragrance of a languorous perfume.

The man on the bed looked at her in silence for a moment. '*Christo!*' he breathed. 'Each day you are more beautiful.'

'Did you disturb my *siesta* to tell me what I already know?' the girl demanded petulantely.

'If your soul had one tenth the beauty of your body even the Vulture would worship at your feet, die for you.'

La Diablesa shrugged. 'Several have,' she remarked; then her tones changed. There was a quiet ferocity in them that chilled me. 'It was my body you wanted,' she said. 'You stole it, but you know nothing of my soul, nor ever shall; that is not for you. Why did you send for me?'

'I am going to sleep. This is *Señor* Lafitte. Give orders that he has food and a place to sleep, a room near mine. I have already given orders that he is not to be molested if he does not attempt to leave the compound. Later I shall decide what is to be done with him.'

'I have already decided,' I said.

They both looked at me in surprise. 'Yes?' inquired the Vulture. 'And what have you decided?'

'I am going to join your outfit.'

The Vulture regarded me with a half smile. 'I had been thinking of that,' he said, 'but there will be time to discuss it more seriously after we are better acquainted. Go with *La Diablesa* now, and see that I am not disturbed until I call.'

I followed the girl from the room out onto the porch, and from there she led the way to a bedroom a short distance from that occupied by the Vulture. 'Here is your room,' she said. 'The boy is preparing lunch now; it will be ready in about half an hour.' She appraised me indolently and without interest as she spoke. My uniform had been soaked with sea water and slept in until it presented a sorry appearance; I had not shaved for two weeks. Only a welfare worker might have found me interesting. Even on such short acquaintance I could not imagine *La Diablesa* as a welfare worker.

As she turned to leave, I stopped her. 'Would it be possible for me to get a bath and a razor and, perhaps, a change of clothing?' I did not imagine it possible, but there was no harm in asking.

'There is a bath there,' she said, pointing to a door, 'and I'll get you one of the Vulture's razors and a suit of his pajamas. After lunch Kao can clean up your clothes.'

In a few minutes she returned with the things, a razor and a suit of flowered silk pajamas, probably loot from one of the Vulture's piratical ventures. As hungry as I was, the thought of a bath and a shave appealed to me even more than the thought of food. The bathroom was a crude affair, a small room with a plank floor draining toward a hole at the back, where the water ran out onto the ground outside the house, a barrel of water, a small foot tub, and a dipper to dip the water out of the barrel; there was nothing fancy about the appointments, but the water was wet and there was soap. With that combination a man can get a bath.

A half hour later, when I came out on the porch again, I felt like a million dollars; but I was hungrier than ever. The girl was in the hammock, reading. She did not look up. 'The kitchen is at the far end of the porch,' she said. 'Kao must have something ready by this time.'

As I passed around in front of the hammock she glanced at me; and I noticed a sudden, new interest alter the expression of surliness that had seemed habitual to her. Perhaps it was the shave. 'Wait a minute,' she said. 'I feel a little hungry myself. If Kao's ready, I'll eat with you.'

We walked the length of the porch together and into a small dining room. The table was laid with a white cloth and with beautiful glassware and silver, but it was laid for only one.

La Diablesa clapped her hands, and a Chinese poked his head through a doorway. 'Is luncheon ready, Kao?' asked the girl.

'All ready,' replied the man, eyeing me furtively and with some surprise.

'Then lay another place for *Señor* Lafitte.'

As I drew back her chair, *La Diablesa* shot a quick glance at me, and a peculiar expression crossed her countenance. She seated herself with a short little laugh. 'I have been unaccustomed to such courtesies for a long time,' she said.

I could think of no comment to make as I walked around the table and seated myself opposite her, and there was a strained silence for several moments.

'That food smells good,' I said, as a whiff of spicy cooking was wafted into the dining room. 'I haven't had a good meal for two weeks, and practically nothing at all for the last few days. I feel as though I could eat a cow, horns and all. But at that it's great to have an appetite, provided of course that one has the means to satisfy it.'

'We live fairly well here most of the time,' offered the girl, 'and Kao's a splendid cook.'

'You have lived here a long time?' I asked.

'Two years,' she replied, 'but it seems like ten.'

'Of course you get away occasionally for trips?' I suggested.

She shook her head. 'I haven't been off the damned island since I came here.'

'Don't you accompany your husband to Singapore or Manila?'

'Husband!' She laughed again, that strange, short laugh. 'You mean the Vulture?'

I nodded.

'What made you think we were married?'

'Your conversation didn't sound much like lover's,' I reminded her with a smile.

Again that laugh. 'The Vulture doesn't marry his women.'

Her reply left me a trifle embarrassed. I couldn't seem to find just the right thing to say under the circumstances, if there was a right thing; so I concentrated my attention on the food for a few moments. When I chanced to glance up at her again she was looking at me.

'Do you know,' she remarked, 'that when I first saw you I thought you were just another beachcomber?' She laughed in a natural, pleasant sort of way this time. 'But now that you are shaved and cleaned up you are quite good-looking, aren't you?'

'I have never taken any prizes for it.'

She laughed again. 'I think we are going to be good friends.

It is a relief to have somebody around who is human. With the exception of Kao, these men here are all beasts.'

'If you don't like it here, why don't you leave?'

'Leave! I shall never leave; I shall be buried out there in the jungle . . . with his other women . . . you and I both, *Señor* Lafitte. When he tires of me, or sees another he prefers, *s-s-st!*' She drew a slim forefinger quickly across her white throat from ear to ear with gruesome significance. 'The Vulture does not believe in wasting ammunition on women.'

'He didn't seem such a fiend,' I remarked meditatively. 'From his speech, I thought him rather a gentleman than a ruffian.'

'He has the culture of a gentleman, and many of his tastes are refined,' replied the girl. 'For example, these table appointments. He loves such refinements. His Spanish and his French are almost those of a scholar; his manner, when he wishes, is that of a grandee of Spain. But at heart he is a fiend.

'At nineteen he was an officer in the navy of Spain. Because of a scandal he was either forced to resign or was cashiered; then he joined the merchant marine. He was second mate of a small cargo steamer when he led a mutiny and with his own hands murdered the captain and first mate. After that, of course, he was an outlaw. Piracy was about the only profession open to a man with his training and in his position.'

'Isn't it rather odd that the authorities have never apprehended him?' I asked.

'The mutiny was so long ago that it is probably all but forgotten,' she explained. 'Of the original mutineers only one returned to civilization; it is what this man may have told that causes the Vulture the only fear of retribution that he feels. All of the other mutineers but one are dead; that one fellow is a called the Portuguese. It was he whom they were fighting on the beach today.

'The Portuguese and the Vulture worked together for many years. Together, they saw to it that their fellow mutineers were done away with. Ten years ago they quarreled and separated. The Portuguese stole a fortune in pearls and gold and jewels from the Vulture and established his headquarters on an island about a hundred miles to the northeast, and the two have been at war constantly since.

'The Portuguese is a miser; he hoards his loot, disposing

of only enough to give him the funds he requires for new equipment. And that is little enough, since he is able to steal practically everything he requires.

'Two weeks ago he struck the Vulture a serious blow. No one knew he was within a hundred miles of the island when, one night, he slipped into the harbor and captured the Vulture's ship, killing five of the Vulture's men who formed the watch aboard. Then he ran the vessel out to sea and stood off the coast until morning, so that the Vulture could see what he was doing; then he sank the ship in full view of us. Today, he came to finish what he had started. The Portuguese has his own ideas about dealing with competition.'

'Being an American, I can't say that they're particularly original,' I commented. 'But they're certainly effective, if they work.'

'He would have killed us all and added the Vulture's loot to his. There is no telling what his own treasure is worth now; but the Vulture has told me that it must run into the millions, as he has been hoarding it for nearly twenty years.'

'And the Vulture has as much?' I asked.

'Oh, no; he is a spender. But he has plenty at that. He showed me a handful of pearls only recently, the smallest of which must be worth over two thousand pounds; and in addition he has coin and plate and jewels.'

Kao had been padding back and forth between the kitchen and the dining room; and while *La Diablesa* talked I had been eating and thinking, too, while I listened. I could not help but wonder what train of circumstances had deposited this girl on this lonely island, the mistress of a thieving cut-throat. Her speech, her manner, everything about her seemed so foreign to her present status that she presented an enigma that piqued my curiosity.

She seemed so friendly and communicative that I thought I might venture to ask her, and I did.

'I am not here of my own will,' she replied. 'It is not much of a story, and I doubt that it would interest you.'

'I am sure that it would, if you care to tell me,' I assured her. 'You see, you interest me very much; and we have something in common; I am not here of my own will either. From what you have told me, we are both prisoners with the same unpleasant fate to look forward to.'

'But you have one advantage.'

'What is that?' I asked.

'The Vulture will not make love to you.' She shuddered as she spoke. 'Love! I have come to hate it.'

'Sometimes it brings unhappiness; but not always, I suppose.'

'It has brought me only unhappiness,' she said, bitterly. 'Once I thought that I was in love. It was while I was still in the convent where I was educated. He was a beautiful young man. I saw him to talk with alone but once; then my father heard of it, and he was furious. He had other plans. He was rich, but our family was nothing. He had ambitions for me; so he married me off to an old man who had family but no money. I guess he was a nice old man; but *mon dieu!* he was so old, and I was only sixteen. We lived just outside Paris, near my father.

'That year! It was awful. My husband had asthma and rheumatism, he walked with two canes; but his family was one of the oldest in France. He often mentioned this fact to me, but I could not believe that even his family was as old as he. He said he was sixty years old, but he had a granddaughter who was over thirty.

'My father persuaded him that a sea voyage would help his asthma and insisted that we take his yacht and cruise in southern waters. My husband had been reading about the beautiful girls in the south sea islands and decided that we should cruise there. Why are old men like that?'

I shook my head. 'I do not know; I am not that old yet.'

La Diablesa laughed. 'He was so old, but he still had his eyes and his imagination,' she shrugged, and 'there he ended.

'It was a long voyage, and it did not help his asthma. Also, he never saw a beautiful island girl, not one. Poor old man! Sometimes I almost weep even now when I think of him. He traveled so far, and for what? Death.

'One day a little schooner hailed us. Her captain said that he was a pearler, and that he was out of water. The captain of our yacht told him to come aboard and he would let him have water; so the pearler lowered a boat, and with six men in it it came alongside. They all clambered over the side, making their boat fast with a line. One of them was a white man – it was the Vulture. But of course we knew nothing of what that meant, even if we had known who he was.

'But we were not left long in ignorance. My husband and I were sitting on deck. I was looking at the strangers, and I did not like the looks of them. They made me afraid. I had never seen such villainous-looking men in all my life, but the presence of the white man reassured me. Then he caught sight of me, and a new light flared in his eyes.

'What happened during the next few minutes aboard that beautiful white yacht was, I know, most horrible though today I cannot seem ever to visualize it as that little convent-reared bride must have. Today the horror has gone out of it; it only seems messy.

'At a word from the Vulture his men whipped revolvers and cutlasses from beneath their sarongs. They shot down the captain first. The Vulture strode to where I stood trembling at my husband's side. He cut the old man's throat. They killed us all. Yes, even the little convent bride was killed; but a new woman was born. Out of that bloody womb of cruelty and lust and avarice *La Diablesa* came into the world.

'Won't you have some more shrimp? Or may I have Kao bring you another cup of coffee?'

Chapter Nine

SECOND IN COMMAND

FOR A MONTH the Vulture hovered between life and death. There was no one in his house who loved him; there were at least two who might have felt safer had he died; yet every effort was made to nurse him back to health. Thus do the personalities of some men dominate even though their bodies may no longer enforce their wills. The Vulture stood weak and helpless upon the verge of eternity, and none dared push him over the brink.

I wandered about the compound as it suited me, and came to know all of the Vulture's cutthroats by name. After I picked up the weird pidgin language that they used and a smattering of Malay, the Vulture often used my services to transmit orders and obtain reports from his chief lieutenants, of which there were two, Ludang and Sato.

Ludang was a surly Eurasian, part Portuguese, part native. He had been with the Vulture for more than ten years and had a bloody record that made him both respected and feared among the vicious brutes that composed the following of the Vulture.

Sato was a full-blooded Japanese, a cruel and crafty fellow whose shrewd and cunning mind constituted his greatest value to the band, though his proficiency with the kris and the mercilessness of his disposition probably went further toward assuring his authority than his mental abilities.

These two were, I think, slightly jealous of one another; and with them the Vulture adopted a tact and diplomacy that he did not bother to waste on others; a fact which convinced me that he placed high value on their services.

I made no effort to fraternize with them or with any other members of the band, and I left their women strictly alone, paying not the slightest attention to them. These, their women, were a wretched lot. Lured from the brothels of Singapore or salvaged from the prizes that the band had captured and sunk, they included Chinese, Japanese, Malays, Filippinos, and dark-skinned Klings and Tamils. They seldom smiled, nor had they much to make them smile other than the rum that they consumed; and that, more often, made them quarrel. All that they had to look forward to was a slit throat when they no longer pleased their lords and masters, which was nothing at all to laugh about.

As the Vulture improved he sent for me more often, and it was soon obvious that he enjoyed my company. 'I get lonely,' he once confessed, 'with no one to talk to. My men, even if I would fraternize with them, are a lot of ignorant beasts who can talk about nothing but rum, women, and murder; and *La Diablesa hates me* – there is no pleasure talking with *La Diablesa*. But then,' he added, 'I did not bring her here just to talk to. She serves her purpose; and I thank the Lord that she is not like most women, who talk too much.'

He looked at me closely for a moment and his cruel eyes narrowed. 'She talks more with you, I have noticed; I often hear you out on the porch. Be sure that you only *talk* with *La Diablesa*.'

That made me laugh. 'Why do you laugh?' he demanded.

'I am not a fool,' I said.

'It is well for you that you are not; and don't get foolish. Women have a way of making fools of men, especially good-looking men.'

'Don't worry.'

'It is for you to worry, not me.' He regarded me in silence for a moment. 'I have been wondering what to do with you. There are several reasons why I would rather not kill you. In the first place, I enjoy your company; then, it always goes against my grain to let this scum see me kill a white man. It is bad for their morale and bad for my position among them. I've always to keep the fallacy of white superiority clearly in their minds. I learned that from the English. That is why I never associate with any members of my crew; I am always master and they are always servants. If you live, you must adopt the same policy.'

The matter of fact way in which he discussed the possibility of my early demise interested me strangely. 'I hope you will let me know if you decide to kill me,' I ventured.

'It presents a problem,' he announced seriously. 'I cannot take you into my service as an ordinary member of the crew; that would lower my prestige as a white. You could only be second in command; it would not do to have you taking orders even from Ludang or Sato. But if I put you over Ludang and Sato . . . ' He shook his head. 'It takes a real man to get obedience from those two; and you have no background; you have never done anything.'

'My murders are few and inconsequential,' I admitted; 'I have been handicapped by lack of opportunity.'

He looked at me through narrowed lids. 'I have tried not to develop my sense of humor.' he said. 'I learned that, too, from the English; they have been a very successful race. I advise you to emulate them.'

A moment later he dismissed me, saying that he wished to sleep; and as I was going to my room *La Diablesa* came from hers. 'How is he?' she asked, nodding in the direction of the Vulture's quarters.

'He's getting along all right,' I replied. 'I think he's out of danger.'

She grimaced. 'I hoped he would die.'

'Don't forget that he has given orders that you are to die if he does,' I reminded her.

'The Vulture alive is one thing, the Vulture dead is another; they might not obey a dead vulture. If he lives, I am sure to die; so I would prefer taking the other chance. And then there is you.'

'What have I to do with it?'

She came very close, so close that her body touched mine, and looked up into my face. 'You would not let them kill me, would you . . . Jean?' The way she pronounced my name was almost a caress. I thought of what the Vulture had just said to me: 'Women have a way of making fools of men.'

I laughed and was about to make some joking reply when her hand touched mine. What is there in that contact of flesh and flesh that awakens funny little devils in a man's breast? Hot, palpitating little devils that race through all his veins. I did not love *La Diablesa*, but I wanted to take her in my arms and tell her that I loved her.

She stood there looking up into my eyes, her warm body against mine, her eyes half closed. My lips were dropping slowly but surely towards hers when she turned away. Humming a gay little tune, she walked over to her hammock. It was the first time I had heard song in the throat of *La Diablesa.*

As I followed her across the porch, Ludang came hurriedly into the patio. He was heading for the Vulture's quarters when I stopped him. 'Don't go in there,' I said. 'He is asleep.'

He gave me a scowl. 'It is important,' he said, but I noticed that he did not go on toward the room.

'What is it?' I demanded. 'If it's important, I'll wake him; otherwise, I'll tell him about it later.'

Ludang's scowling face would have curdled milk. I could see that he wanted to ignore me, but evidently the Vulture had implanted within his breast too well the idea of white supremacy. 'There is a schooner offshore,' he said. 'She is working her way toward the harbor.' They always referred to the little cove that afforded them a safe anchorage as the harbpr.

'Is it the Portuguese?' I asked.

'No, it's an English yacht.'

'I'll go down and have a look at her,' I said. 'Get the men together and wait for me in the compound.' He was about to demur. He hesitated. 'And be quick about it!' Our eyes met; his were filled with challenge and rebellion. I just stood and waited as though I expected him to obey me, but my eyes never left his; and finally they shifted to one side and then dropped. Almost simultaneously he turned away and walked toward the compound. I had won.

As I turned to go to my room for my gun and ammunition belt I saw *La Diablesa* standing looking at me; the light in her eyes was almost ecstatic. 'Bravo!' she whispered as I passed her. 'Now I know I need no longer fear the Vulture.'

'Keep your powder dry nevertheless,' I cautioned her.

Either she did not understand the allusion or had more confidence in my prowess than her experience of me warranted, for she followed me into my room. She had never been in there before. Both of us knew that if the Vulture learned of it someone would die.

As I buckled on my gun, *La Diablesa* stood staring at me. I was in a hurry and was moving toward the door as I adjusted the cartridge belt. *La Diablesa* stepped in front of me; her lips were raised toward mine. 'Just once, Jean, before you go!'

I swept her into my arms and crushed her to me; as my lips covered hers her eyes closed and she hung limp in my embrace. At first I thought she had swooned; but she hadn't, and I quickly disengaged myself and hurried toward the compound.

Here I found nearly a score of lowering browed gallows birds clustered behind Ludang and Sato. Evidently the two had been discussing the propriety of taking orders from me, for when I started toward the main gate and told them to follow me Ludang stepped in front of me and barred my way. He had a mighty ugly look in his eyes.

'Not so fast!' he exclaimed. 'We take our orders from the Vulture, not from you.'

I realized that this was no time to temporize. If I were ever to be second in command to the Vulture, now was the time and this the opportunity to prove my right to authority over this choice band of murderers; and I had sense enough to know that conversation was not the persuasive force with which to sway these dim intellects. Furthermore, I had already decided that I would be second in command.

Ludang was in my way. He stood there with one hand on the hilt of his kris. I swung a right to his jaw that dropped him in his tracks; then I faced them with my gun.

'I am giving orders for the Vulture,' I said. 'Get up, Ludang. You and Sato go ahead to the beach, the rest of us will follow. Keep out of sight of the schooner until I get a look at her.'

Ludlang scrambled to his feet. Holy mackerel, but he was mad! He hesitated just an instant, looking at the business end of my .45 Official Police; and then he turned toward the gate, and Sato followed him.

As I threaded that narrow jungle trail with those other devils at my back I was not exactly what one might call carefree; but I didn't dare let them guess that I anticipated anything but obedience from them. And so I never gave them even a backward glance, though I must admit that I gave them many a backward thought. Presently I heard some of them laughing, and then I knew that I was safe as far as they were concerned; they were enjoying the discomfiture of Ludang.

The Eurasian and the Japanese halted at the edge of the jungle at the summit of the cliff above the beach, and when I joined them I saw a beautiful schooner-yacht just lowering anchor in the cove. She carried the British colors, and she offered an avenue of escape; but these facts seemed to make no impression upon my consciousness such as they should have. Something had happened to me; I had undergone a metamorphosis that had produced a man that was not I. My new psychology was not that of the peace officer or the embryo attorney; it was the psychology of old Jean Lafitte, the corsair of the Gulf of Mexico. I looked upon that trim craft with the eyes of a pirate.

I turned to Ludang. 'Have you a small boat?' I asked.

'It is hidden in a cave at the end of the beach,' he replied surlily.

'Can five men launch it?'

'Yes.'

'You and Sato take three men and get her into the water; we are going to board the schooner and take her.'

'With five men?' asked Sato.

'With six; I am going with you, of course. If we take a boat load of men they will suspect something, and they may put up a fight before we can get aboard.'

Sato grinned and nodded. He called three men by name from those behind me. I told the others to remain out of sight; then the six of us walked down the narrow trail to the beach. I saw some people aboard the yacht watching us as we walked toward the cave where the small boat was hidden. The distance was too great for me to be able to recognize any details of dress or color, and so I doubted that they could discern us any better. I had the men hide their weapons as best they could, for I guessed that someone aboard the schooner would have glasses on us shortly.

After the boat was launched, I took my place in the bow; for I wanted to be the first aboard the prize. I can't tell you why, there was just a feeling in me that I must be first. It was not bravado, nor any desire to impress the men of my party. It seemed to be something that was necessary, like using the right fork at dinner.

Now I saw a man on the deck of the schooner with glasses at his eyes. I wondered what he thought of us. We must all have looked about alike. My skin was as dark as that of many of the men with me. I have always been much out of doors in the California sunshine, and the wind and exposure to which my calling had subjected me had given me the hue of a Hawaiian. I was clothed in shorts and a cotton shirt, and because the shirt tails were too short I had wrapped a red sash around my waist to cover the discrepancy. Another piece of red cloth was wound about my head to take the place of my cap that had blown into the Pacific weeks before. I did not realize it at the time, but I must have looked every inch a pirate from the deck of that schooner.

We were about a hundred yards from the yacht when we were hailed. There were about a dozen men on deck leaning over the rail watching us. One of them was a white man; the others appeared to be natives. I saw the white speak to a native standing beside him, and the latter hailed us.

'Who are you, and what do you want?' he called.

I turned to Ludang and told him what to answer. 'We are shipwrecked sailors,' shouted Ludang, 'and we want to come aboard.'

I understood all that was said, but it was evident that the white man on the deck of the yacht did not, for the man who had hailed us turned and repeated Ludang's words, translating them, I imagined, into English.

It was then, for the first time, that I noticed that the white man carried a rifle. It had been hidden behind the rail; but now he swung it to his shoulder and fired, all with such rapidity that no one could have prevented his unexpected attack. He had fired point-blank at us, and we were too close for me to entertain any hope that he had missed a whole boat-load of men. I did not turn to see, nor did I need to. A sudden stifled cry from behind me followed by an oath and a groan, told the story.

It takes so long to put such things on paper that one might gather the idea that I stood there for minutes after one of my men was shot, gawping at the marksman on the yacht; but I didn't. I think I have mentioned elsewhere that I was a good rifle shot when I was a member of the R.O.T.C. Since joining the police force I had perfected my work with the revolver until I could shoot in such company as that of Davis of the Los Angeles Police Department and not feel ashamed of myself. I prided myself particularly on my draw.

The fellow on the schooner had taken us all by surprise, but at that he squeezed his trigger only a fraction of a split second before I squeezed mine. It was a long pistol shot; and perhaps I was lucky, but the fellow slumped across the rail with a bullet hole between his eyes before he had the satisfaction of seeing the effect of his own shot.

Ludang, at my shoulder, let out a great oath of appreciation. Then I fired again and another man fell. 'Bend to your oars, you bastards!' I shouted to the men behind me. 'Ludang and I will fire while you row.'

Ludang fired once and then I told him to hold his fire until I had emptied my gun, after which he was to fire while I reloaded. My third shot brought down another man, and then the balance scampered for cover, but I winged one more before they all got out of sight.

Sato had taken the place at the oar of the man who had been shot, and there was a fellow sculling in the stern. They were doing the best they could, but the boat was rather cumbersome for three oars, and our progress seemed painfully slow.

For a minute or two, now, there was no sign of life aboard the schooner; and then I heard the *putt-putt* of a motor; they had started the auxiliary. There was a gentle sea breeze which kept the schooner swinging at her anchor with her nose pointed straight to sea, and I suppose some damn fool thought that by starting the auxiliary they could just *putt-putt* out to sea, dragging their anchor. It was evident that no one relished the idea of taking a trick at the wheel under our fire.

Of course, as soon as the vessel got under way she began describing a circle about the anchor. It was a ragged sort of circle, for the anchor would drag a little way first in one direction and then in another; but it always caught and held enough to swing her stern around to a new direction.

We were getting closer now, and those on board were getting more and more desperate. They had to do something and do it in a hurry; so they made a sortie from below. A few, with firearms, hid behind the deckhouse or the masts and peppered away at us; one made a dash for the wheel, and a couple for the capstan. If they could get the anchor aweigh before we overhauled them, they could show us a clean pair of heels with the little *putt-putt*.

Of course I couldn't take a chance on this; so I dropped the two men who were trying to up anchor. Ludang grunted in admiration, although he probably hated my guts; but I was doing something that he could understand and appreciate.

'Shoot at those birds behind the masts,' I told him. 'I'll take care of the deckhouse bunch.'

Their shots had been going wild before, and now that we were concentrating on their positions, they almost stopped; with bullets crashing close every time they poked their heads out to see their target they became more cautious. The man at the wheel was harmless, so I didn't bother with him; and after he saw the two at the capstan drop he got down on his belly and crawled away to cover.

As we were running in under the bow of the schooner I reloaded my gun and slipped it into its holster; then, with the aid of the bobstays and the bowsprit, I clambered to the deck of the yacht. Ludang, who had quickly made the small boat fast to one of the bobstays, followed me; and the others swarmed over the bow in our wake.

A bullet whizzed by my ear as I ran aft. It came from the

rifle of the fellow behind the foremast, and before he could duck back out of sight I dropped him. Now, the others fell back. It was a mixed crew: a Negro, a Chinaman, a couple of half-breeds, and two Malays, as nearly as I could judge; these were what was left.

The Negro was the first to throw down his gun. As he did so he shoved his hands above his head; then the others followed his example. It didn't help them any. The only result was to save us a little ammunition. Those sweet babies behind me just shoved their guns into their belts and drew their krises; the rest was merely butchery. When they were through the deck was a shambles. Then I ordered them to search the schooner.

'If there are women aboard, bring them to me; do not harm them.' Somehow I felt that they would obey me, but I prayed that there were no women on the yacht. When Sato returned and reported that there was no one below I breathed a sigh of relief.

None of my men knew anything about motors, so I took charge of that as well as commanding the ship. Inasmuch as I had never been aboard a vessel before except in the capacity of passenger, I was not exactly sure of myself; but I determined to bluff it through.

We ran out to sea a short distance and dumped the bodies overboard where Sato assured me the prevailing winds and current would not carry them back to the beach; then we returned to the cove and anchored.

The member of our band that the white man had shot had died, and we had thrown his body into the sea with the others; but you may be assured that none was so disposed of before my companions had stripped it of every article of clothing or adornment that had the slightest value.

As we returned to the beach in the small boat we saw the balance of the Vulture's brood waiting on the beach. After we had engaged the schooner they had come down out of their concealment in the jungle and watched the affair from the beach. They were as enthusiastic as rooters at a football game; and I could tell by a subtle change in their attitude toward me that my position, as far as they were concerned, was assured. I say assured, but nothing was assured in that company save treachery and death. A man could hold his position among them solely by bluff and brutality, and he must have the guts to back up his bluff.

I sent a party of six men, under Ludang, to guard our prize against the possibility of another raid by the Portuguese; then I returned to the stronghold with the remainder.

As I entered the small patio on which my quarters opened, *La Diablesa* met me at the gate. 'The Vulture is waiting for you,' she said in a low tone, 'but don't go near him yet. He is furious. After he learned that you had left the building and gone to the beach he swore to kill you.'

'He'll get over that,' I remarked as I started toward his quarters.

'Please don't go in there now, Jean,' she begged; 'he'll kill you.'

'He doesn't know yet that I'm second in command,' I told her, with a grin, 'and I want to tell him about it.' Then I resumed my way to the Vulture's bedroom.

Chapter Ten

BETRAYED

AS I STEPPED into the doorway of his room, the Vulture reached for a revolver lying on a taboret beside his bed; but I had him covered before his hand could close on it.

'Cut that!' I snapped. 'Don't make a damn fool of yourself.'

His evil eyes regarded me for a moment, his hand still poised above the gun's grip; then slowly his hand dropped to the mattress. He was very angry, but he controlled his voice when he spoke; the hereditary poise of good breeding was often apparent in him at moments like these.

'You disobeyed my orders,' he said, coldly. 'I told you that you would be killed if you left the compound.'

'As second in command, I shall use my judgment in cases of emergency,' I replied.

'Who says you are second in command?' he demanded.

'I do, and so will you.'

The line of his thin lips altered ever so slightly; it might have been a smile. 'And what was the emergency?' he asked.

'A schooner was entering the cove.'

He raised himself on an elbow. '*¡Jesús Cristo y Maria!*' he ejaculated. 'And here I am in bed! Is she still there?'

'Yes.'

'Send Ludang to me! Hurry! A ship sent by heaven; and I lying here in bed, and no one to take her for me. Send Ludang!'

'Ludang is not here.'

'Not here!' he cried. 'Where is he?'

'He is aboard the schooner. I left him there in charge of six men to guard her.'

'*You* left him there! What did you have to do with it?'

'I told you once that I am second in command; I captured the schooner for you.'

He eyed me intently for a long time. 'You took it alone?' he asked.

'Of course not,' I replied. 'I had Ludang, Sato, and three others with me. One of them was killed. Didn't you hear the shooting?'

'No; the jungle cuts off sounds from the harbor. And they obeyed you? Ludang and Sato?'

'Certainly. They weren't keen about it at first; but after I knocked Ludang down and got the drop on Sato and the others, they came to their senses.'

'You knocked Ludang down and you are here alive?'

'Yes; and you have a ship again, an auxiliary schooner-yacht. I don't know much about ships, but she looks pretty sweet to me.'

'And they obeyed you! What did you tell them?'

'I told them that while you were laid up they'd take orders from me.'

'And they obeyed you!' He kept repeating that as though it were some sort of miracle that was beyond his understanding.

'Well, how about it?' I demanded.

'How about what?'

'Am I second in command?'

'I didn't know that there was any longer any doubt of it,' he replied.

'There wasn't in my mind,' I assured him, 'but I thought you might still entertain doubts.'

'No,' he said, 'but be careful when you disobey my orders that you are always in the right. Tell Kao to bring a bottle of champagne and a couple of glasses; we must drink to this,' and as I was going out the door, 'Make it three glasses and call *La Diablesa.*'

The Vulture didn't mend very rapidly. He'd be up for a while and overdo; then he'd have to go back to bed again. He was up and down like that for more than a year, and he never got farther than the beach and that only once.

He had wanted to see the new schooner; so I had a chair rigged up and a couple of the men carried him down. He never enthused about anything, but I could see that he liked her. The exertion was too much for him; the wound re-opened, and he came near dying during the next few weeks, but he pulled through.

During that year I sailed the *Señorita*, as the Vulture christened the new vessel, up and down lonely seas. We had disguised her so effectually that her builder wouldn't have known her, and we sailed as honest pearlers. We did fairly well, making at least two big hauls. One was a pearler that had made a lucky strike; the other a little tramp that was taking a rich Chinese back home. He had turned all his property into gold and had it with him. Where we sent him, he wouldn't need it; so we took it.

I took a few prisoners, likely-looking fellows whom I thought we might use to fill vacancies, for we didn't always come out unscathed; we lost five men during those first cruises of mine. We slit the throats of those we didn't want and dumped their bodies into the sea. I didn't like to do it, but there was no other way. Had we set a single man ashore we'd have had a couple of navies after us in no time. Our only safety lay in sinking without trace.

To some it may seem a dirty business, but I am not writing this to win converts or sympathy. I believe that an auto-biography should tell the truth; otherwise there is no possible excuse for writing one. What good this one will do I do not know. As a matter of fact I do not really know why I am writing it. I do not need the money it will bring, if it sells. I am offering no excuses for the things I have done. I hold no brief for piracy.

I believe that I was born a pirate; and that accident provided the means by which I might express my individuality, fulfill my destiny. I have done so without shame and without hypocrisy. Other men are born pirates, but they go into business or the professions. I hold them in contempt. At least I shall not feel it incumbent upon me in my old age to give away bright new dimes to assuage the flagellation of my conscience.

I have killed men, but I have never sent their widows large bills for my operations. I have robbed people of their all, but I have mercifully put them out of their misery that they might not live to bemoan their losses or suffer the deprivations and reproaches of poverty. In my own way I too am a philanthropist and a benefactor of the human race.

One thing I could never do and never have done; I could not kill women or children. I took them back to the island with me. At first the Vulture stormed around and ordered them all killed. But he was in bed, and I was up; for the time at least my authority was greater than his. I had my way, and later I convinced him that I was right.

I put the women and the older children at work clearing more ground around the stronghold and planting crops. All the boys over eight were trained in seamanship and the use of weapons. From the beginning they were taught that they were being trained to be pirates, and I began immediately to instill a code of ethics into their young minds; it consisted principally in undying loyalty to the chief, and I gave them to understand that *I* was their chief. The women and girls were to be used to breed more pirates.

The Vulture eventually got back into harness, but I had been virtual chief for so long that I didn't enjoy playing second fiddle. I determined, therefore, that at the first opportunity I would pick a quarrel with the Vulture and kill him; but first I wanted to get enough of my own men men aboard the *Señorita* to handle the men of the old crew who might prove too loyal to their chief. I considered as my men those whose lives I had spared, in whose minds I had sought to implant the suggestion that I was their protector and their friend.

But there was also another reason for wanting to get rid of

the Vulture; I had begun to suspect that he was entertaining the suspicion that my relations with *La Diablesa* had gone beyond the conversational stage. All her life *La Diablesa* had been starved for love, and she was having difficulty in hiding her attachment to me. She liked to be caressed, and I knew that it was only a matter of time before the Vulture would come upon us unexpectedly. That might prove both embarrassing and lethal.

The Vulture's thoughts were partially distracted from contemplation of *La Diablesa*'s indiscretion by certain rumors that had been coming to our ears from the prisoners I had spared. Throughout that vast network of islands gossip circulates with remarkable, almost uncanny rapidity, especially gossip from the big centers like Singapore; and so the fame of a certain courtesan of that unholy city was upon many a tongue.

She was reported to be a mysterious white woman of unbelievable beauty, who had come from none knew where. None of those who spoke of her had seen her; she was not for such as they; but they described her charms as intimates might, and apparently the less they knew of her the more glowing were their descriptions.

I knew nothing of Singapore at that time, and so I visualized the girl as something of a glorified night club hostess. That she queened it over some den of iniquity might readily be postulated from all the evidence that filtered to us through the sea scum that were our prisoners; also, it was apparent that her favors were for white men alone, the richest and the highest placed.

The Vulture was interested. He had not tired of *La Diablesa*; but he had, I am sure, begun to doubt her. The more he thought of this mysterious woman the more his imagination was inflamed. It was now about two years since I had joined him, and he had not been to Singapore during that time; so he was doubly anxious to have a vacation.

The plan that I had inaugurated, which the Vulture called a breeding farm for pirates, necessitated that someone with authority remain always on the island. Ludang, he wanted with him, Sato, he could not trust; so he informed me one day that while he was gone upon his vacation to Singapore I should remain in charge at the island.

I didn't like the idea, for I wanted to see Singapore; likewise, I knew that the inaction and monotony of a couple of months on the island would bore me to extinction. The only bright spot in the outlook was the fact that I should have *La Diablesa*'s undivided company. She was a bright, cultured girl; and I enjoyed being with her. Environment had probably changed her greatly, yet underneath she was still sweet and womanly. The contrasting reactions of heredity and environment were, however, sometimes most startling. She might be considering my comfort with the deepest feminine solicitude at the very moment that she was urging me to murder the Vulture.

Really, to neither of us did there seem anything essentially immoral in this latter suggestion; it was only when I attempted to square it with the standards of that other world from which I had come that it seemed startling. But those standards were slipping into the background, becoming less definite each day.

The day before the Vulture was to sail I was out inspecting the garden patches that were being worked by the women and children, when I saw him going toward the beach with Ludang and several of his crew. He was a practical and efficient man, and I knew that he was going down to the *Señorita* to make a final check of her equipment and provisions before sailing in the morning. Not having found me in my quarters he had assumed that I was on the ship. During recent months he had been careful to see that *La Diablesa* and I were never left alone together, or at least so it had seemed to me.

When I had finished my inspection, I walked back to the house. *La Diablesa* was lying in her hammock just as I had seen her that first time two years before. At the sound of my step she looked up, and when she recognized me she arose and stood awaiting me. Her expression was very sad and almost frightened.

'What is the matter, dear?' I asked.

She threw herself upon me, her arms about my neck, and commenced to sob. It was the first time that I had ever seen *La Diablesa* cry. 'What is it? Tell me,' I urged.

'He is going to take me with him,' she managed to articulate between her sobs. 'I am lost. I shall never see you again. Oh, kill him, Jean! Kill him! Do not let him take me away.'

'It will be only for a month or two,' I reminded her.

'It will be forever,' she replied. 'At this time . . . oh, you *must* understand! Before the two months are past he will kill me, for by then he will know. Only yesterday he told me that I should take better care of my figure, that I was getting too fat.

'And it is not that, alone, Jean; the moment he told me that I was to go with him I knew that he meant that I should never come back. I know him; he is going after that woman he has heard about. If he likes her, he will steal her; and I shall go overboard with my throat slit. It is a presentiment, what you call a hunch. Oh, Jean, don't let him take me!'

I intended killing the Vulture eventually, but I was not ready yet. My colonizing plan had brought about certain complications that I had not foreseen, which made it inexpedient for me to risk the temper of the Vulture's old crew at this time.

Many of them objected strenuously to the considerable increase in the number of the band, which naturally decreased the pro rata share of the loot each would receive. Ludang hated me for many reasons, not the least of which was his own ambition to succeed the Vulture when the latter died. The men upon whom I might count were far less bloodthirsty than those who might be expected to support or avenge the Vulture. These were a few of the conditions that made it highly dangerous to attempt a *coup* at this time.

'Why do you hesitate?' demanded *La Diablesa*. 'Are you afraid?'

'The time is not ripe yet,' I replied. 'And, besides, I think you overestimate the danger. Your condition makes you nervous.'

'I know him so well,' she replied, 'that I find a meaning in his every gesture and expression that others would miss entirely or not understand. He is suspicious, and he is planning something.'

We had been moving very slowly across the porch. Gently. *La Diablesa* guided me toward the door to her own rooms. 'Come inside, Jean,' she suggested. 'There will be less danger that we shall be overheard; and then,' she added, looking up at me with tears in her eyes, 'it may be the last time we shall ever be alone together.'

Beyond the threshold, I took her in my arms. 'Don't

worry; everything will come out all right,' I assured her.

She snuggled closer to me. 'Do you love me?' she asked.

I pressed her closer. Maybe it was the same as telling her that I loved her, something I had never told her in words. I didn't know myself exactly what I felt for *La Diablesa*; perhaps it was only infatuation engendered by propinquity, her beauty, and her own passion. I loved Daisy Juke. I knew that I should never love anyone else in the same way; but I could never have her, for by this time she was married to another man, had been for nearly two years.

'Promise that you will kill him,' she begged.

We were standing in the center of the room; she was facing the open door, toward which my back was turned. Against the opposite wall, and directly in front of me, stood a dressing table above which hung a mirror.

In reply to her I shook my head. 'I am not ready to kill him yet,' I said.

Her right arm was around my neck, her left hand was at my waist, toying with the red sash that girdled my hips. Suddenly I felt her go rigid in my arms, and at the same instant my eyes happened to rest upon the mirror above the dressing table. In it I saw the reflection of the Vulture and Ludang entering the small patio; *La Diablesa* had seen them first over my shoulder. We were in plain sight of them.

La Diablesa must have thought very quickly in that brief instant. She clung to me tightly, so that I could not extricate myself quickly, and commenced to scream for help.

I was so astonished that for a moment I was helpless; then I pushed her aside and turned toward the door. The Vulture and Ludang were running toward me. Well, it had come to a showdown now, and I would have to kill him and Ludang too. I reached for my gun. . . . My holster was empty.

But I scarcely had time to more than just realize that I was unarmed when something heavy hit me on the back of the head, and I fell unconscious to the floor.

Chapter Eleven

OVERBOARD

WHEN I REGAINED consciousness I was on my own bed, and the Vulture was standing a few feet away twirling my gun on his finger. A cigarette was dangling from his thin, cruel lips, the smoke curling about his sinister face. As I opened my eyes I saw him as a vision of the Devil in Hell with the smoke of his eternal fires half veiling his evil countenance.

Slowly my mind cleared, and little by little I recalled what had happened. What I had not actually witnessed, I now guessed. *La Diablesa*, realizing that we were discovered, had sought to make herself appear the unwilling victim of my undesired attentions. Lest her attitude might otherwise seem unconvincing, she had removed my gun from its holster as she stood with her arms about me, and then, as I had whirled about to face the Vulture, she had hit me over the head with it. Either that or else the two had deliberately planned the whole thing.

'I ought to kill you,' said the Vulture.

'Well, why don't you?' I demanded.

'Perhaps I shall later; I need you now. And then,' he added, '*La Diablesa* asked me not to.'

This statement smelled fishy; it was inconsistent with what *La Diablesa* had done to me. That the Vulture would heed such an appeal seemed improbable.

'She must want to finish the job herself,' I ventured.

He smiled his mirthless smile. 'A shrewd guess, my friend. *La Diablesa* begged me to spare you that she might kill you. She is very angry.'

'I underestimated her virtue,' I said.

'So did I,' admitted the Vulture. 'Perhaps that is one reason that I have not killed you already; you have shown me that *La Diablesa* is true to me.'

My head ached and I was facing death, but I almost smiled. 'How could you have doubted it?' I asked.

He tossed my gun onto the bed beside me. 'Go aboard the *Señorita*,' he said, 'and remain there until we sail. You are going with me.' Then he turned and walked from the room. The Vulture was a very brave man.

The following morning, when he came aboard the schooner, *La Diablesa* was not with him. Ludang and the old crew were there however with the exception of Sato. There seemed to be no change in my status; I was still second in command. Kao had been brought along as cook. He gave me his usual friendly smile as he came aboard; but the others seemed even more surly than usual, especially Ludang. I sensed a change toward me. It was as though they feared me less, knowing that I had incurred the displeasure of their chief. Their attitude boded ill. I felt like a lone sheep in a den of wolves, all of which were ready to tear me to pieces the instant that their leader turned on me. I wondered if they were waiting, knowing that he would turn.

'I thought you were bringing *La Diablesa*,' I remarked, as the Vulture joined me.

'I changed my plans,' he replied. 'It occurred to me that it might prove unpleasant to have *La Diablesa* and the other woman on board together. I should have been forced to rid myself of one of them. Now I shall have a chance to get acquainted with the new one before it is necessary to reach a decision. Perhaps I shall find that I prefer *La Diablesa* after all.'

The Vulture was nothing if not practical, even in matters of the heart. He was not going to discard one love before he had acquired and was sure of the next.

Kao told me that had he brought *La Diabelsa* along and found the new girl to his liking, *La Diabelsa* would have gone overboard as soon as the *Señorita* cleared Singapore harbor. Kao was a brimming well of information; he told me a number of things that I think the Vulture would not have thanked him for telling.

The Chinese was devoted to *La Diablesa* and he seemed to have taken a liking to me. He used to sit with me often when I had a night watch and talk about China. He had a family there, but it had been so long since he had seen any of them that I doubt if he missed them any. There were grown sons and daughters and probably grandchildren by this time; his wife still lived, but the only reason Kao could advance for wanting to return to China was his desire to be buried there. About the only subject under the sun that Kao and I did not discuss during those soft, southern nights was the one uppermost in my mind, *La Diablesa.*

It piqued me to realize that *La Diablesa*'s action had hurt me so deeply, for that hurt suggested that I had loved her, whereas I knew perfectly well that I had never loved, and never would love, any other than Daisy Juke. In my mind I compared the two, the flowerlike beauty of Daisy Juke against the sinister sophistication of the Frendh girl. I heard again the innocent chatter of the school girl and the co-ed against the dark background of *La Diablesa*'s constant urging that I kill the Vulture.

La Diablesa! How well her name became her! And yet, though my whole heart was wrapped in the memory of Daisy Juke it was saddened by recollections of the disillusionment *La Diablesa*'s treachery had wrought.

During the voyage to Singapore I had plenty of time to think of Daisy Juke and *La Diablesa* and many other things, for I was left much to my own devices. The cruise was uneventful; we saw few ships and molested none, for the Vulture was pleasure-bent. He fraternized with me far less than formerly; the affair in *La Disablea*'s room had raised an invisible but nonetheless insuperable barrier between us. The attitude of the crew remained all but openly hostile. I did not enjoy the trip, feeling constantly, as I did, that Death stood every watch with me and hovered perhaps even closer when I slept.

But at length we reached our destination and dropped anchor in the inner basin of the harbor of Singapore. About us was the shipping of many nations: rusty old ocean tramps, tankers, passenger liners, dhows manned by Malabarese and Tamils plied between the ships and the quays, and countless sampans carried their passengers to Johnson's Landing or back to their vessels.

I was watching the activity along Collier Quay from the deck of the *Señorita* and looking forward with pleasurable anticipation to my first visit to the city when the Vulture joined me. He had donned his shore clothes and looked very much the aristocrat, notwithstanding the fact that the cut of his garments was a trifle out of date.

'I see that I shall have to get some presentable clothes,' I remarked.

'Why?' he inquired.

'To wear ashore.'

'You are not going ashore.'

I was looking him in the eyes as he spoke, and what I saw there convinced me that the subject was not one that could be profitably discussed; so I made no reply and turned my attention again toward the shore.

'Do not attempt to leave the ship,' said the Vulture crisply. 'Ludang and half the crew will be here, and I have given orders. You understand?'

I nodded. 'Perfectly.'

He said no more but turned away, and presently I saw him going over the side into the sampan that was to bear him to shore. I was disappointed, and I was also angry. But there was still another reaction that I prefer to describe as apprehension, though perhaps, were this not an autobiography, it might be called fear. I had a feeling that something was going to happen to me, something that would be distinctly unpleasant, and that the Vulture was preserving me until it suited his whim to order the consummation of whatever he purposed.

The days dragged as we lay in the steaming port of Singapore a bare eighty miles above the equator. The crew alternated shore leave in two shifts. Most of them were drunk all of the time. At one time half the crew was in jail. I saw little of the Vulture and that little evidenced the fact that he was in a vile humor.

Each time he came aboard I expected that he would bring the girl he had come for, but he never did. At the end of a week he came over the side late one afternoon with a face like a thundercloud. Summoning Ludang, he ordered him to take two men and round up the members of the crew who were ashore. 'We are sailing tonight, he announced.

He burst into a torrent of vituperation from which I gathered that he had searched Singapore for her for a week and had only just learned that the Portuguese had been there and stolen her scarcely a week before we had arrived.

From the way he crowded sail on the *Señorita* after we left Singapore, I guessed that he hoped to overhaul the Portuguese and attempt to take the girl away from him. But though he risked the ship and all our lives in a couple of bad blows we never sighted the quarry.

The Portuguese's stronghold lay on an island about a hundred miles from ours and directly on our return course from Singapore. The Vulture no longer took me into his confidence in any matter, so I did not know his plans. But I suspected that he intended to pursue the Portuguese to his lair and even land in pursuit of him and the girl.

We raised the island about ten o'clock one morning and then lay to until late in the afternoon when we commenced to creep stealthily upon our quarry. The Vulture mustered all hands during the second dogwatch and very briefly gave his instructions. We were to creep up on the island after dark without lights; there were to be no smoking nor talking, no fire in the galley stove.

'There will be no moon tonight,' said the Vulture in conclusion, 'and we can work in close to the cove where their ship lies, without danger of being discovered. We shall find anchorage there in about six fathoms. Three men will be left aboard; the remainder will land with me and give the Portuguese a surprise.

'We shall avoid his ship going in, but returning, we shall take her. During the attack kill everyone except the women. I am after the white woman he stole in Singapore. See that no harm comes to her.'

It had been a hot and sultry day with only a gentle breeze blowing, and the night brought little relief from the heat. I was lying on deck clothed in nothing but a pair of shorts, trying to endure the heat, when I heard the soft shuffling of naked feet approaching, and presently saw the dim figure of a man bulking close in the blackness of the night.

I thought it was a member of the watch and cleared my throat to warn him of my presence so that he wouldn't stumble over me. Whoever it was stopped and leaned down toward me; then a thin voice spoke in a low whisper.

'Who is?' it asked.

'Oh, hello, Kao!' I replied. 'It is I.'

'*S-s-sh!*' he cautioned, as he lay down beside me. 'Not so loud.'

'What's the matter?' I demanded.

'Plenty matter, Fitty. He just talkee Ludang. They killee

you pletty soon. Vulture plenty mad. No take you back to island; aflaid you makee love 'Blessa. You lookee out. Pletty soon Ludang come. You savvy?'

'I savvy, Kao, and thank you. This was mighty decent of you.'

'Me likee you, me likee 'Blessa, 'Blessa likee you – to damn muchee. He find out, he killee me too. You no tell, Fitty?'

'Of course not, Kao. You'd better beat it before someone sees you talking to me.'

'Good-bye, Fitty!' He faded away into the darkness, my only friend among all those cutthroats.

I was unarmed. I had left my gun in my cabin because of the discomfort of wearing the cartridge belt in the intense heat. It had been a careless thing to do, for one never knew at what instant one might need a weapon in that choice company aboard the *Señorita*. But I could soon correct that matter.

I arose and started toward the companionway that led below. Almost immediately I saw the figure of a man approaching me. He saw me at the same instant and hailed me.

'Is that you, *Señor* Lafitte?' The voice was Ludang's.

So, he had come for me! I wanted to gain time to reach my cabin and get my gun; if they were going to kill me I'd take a few of them along to Hell with me. I particularly wanted to take the Vulture and next to him, Ludang. I should have liked to pass him without revealing my identity, but if he suspected that I was trying to elude him he could easily call to the Vulture, who could then get me as I came down the companionway. I knew he wouldn't use a gun on me, for we were probably within pistol-shot sound of the Portuguese's ship. He would knife me when I came close enough, after assuring himself of my identity. Those devils are adepts with knives.

He stopped in front of me barring my way, his suspicions aroused. 'Who are you?' he demanded.

I had to alter my plans. I knew more ways of fighting than he did. Stepping in quickly, I drove my right to his chin, hoping it would knock him out and thus give me time to reach my cabin before he could sound an alarm.

He went down all right and out, too. But at the instant that he dropped I saw another man directly behind him. This fellow sprang for me, and as he did so he called out, 'Here he is! He got Ludang.'

I might have known that the yellow cowards wouldn't come for me alone. I heard the patter of running feet and saw other forms looming in the darkness. I couldn't fight them all with my bare hands. I turned and ran forward. Then I heard the Vulture's voice in a hoarse whisper. 'Get him!' he ordered. 'A gallon of rum to the man that kills him!'

The whole affair was uncanny: the darkness, the silence broken only by the subdued voice of the Vulture, the pattering of naked feet on the deck, the knowledge that I was being hunted down like a mad dog.

As I ran, a figure loomed suddenly in front of me. I dodged it and ran into another. Once again my fist connected with a chin, and as the fellow dropped I ran across the deck to the port side of the ship, thinking that in the darkness I might elude them long enough to work my way back to my cabin. But I was doomed to disappointment: to my left I saw three more figures running forward to intercept me.

Again I turned. This time I ran toward the bow. They were coming after me fast now, apparently the whole ship's company. In low whispers those nearest me were directing the others as to my whereabouts. Directly ahead of me was the bow of the ship, and now the man on watch there came at me on a run. I was completely cornered!

No, not quite. There remained one avenue of escape. Leaping to the rail, I dove into the sea.

Chapter Twelve

THE QUEEN OF DIAMONDS

I HAD HEARD MEN tell harrowing tales of the ferocity of sharks, and I had listened to others who swore that they were harmless. But what the sharks thought about it I did not know. I knew that these waters were infested with the brutes, and from the instant that the sea closed above me I expected to feel terrible jaws close upon me.

My life has been menaced often and in many ways, but I think I was never in a predicament where I felt more hopeless than I did as I swam away from the *Señorita* through those warm, teeming waters. So certain was I that death hovered certain and inescapable that I was almost convinced of the futility and uselessness of even attempting to escape it. But the urge to live is so much a part of every fiber of our beings that almost mechanically I struck out toward the distant shore.

I couldn't see a thing, of course, but I knew the direction of the wind, and so the waves became my guides. I guessed that we were about a mile offshore; if the wind didn't change I felt reasonably confident that I couldn't miss the island, provided, of course, that the sharks missed me.

As minute succeeded minute and no shark dragged me down my hopes arose, though I must admit that they never got very high. The utter loneliness of my situation was perhaps as depressing as the constant menace of the great fish. Once again, as I had while aboard the derelict dirigible, I experienced the sensation of being the sole inhabitant of a lost world.

At first, glancing back over my shoulder, I had seen the outlines of the *Señorita*'s hull bulking dimly behind me. But soon even that was lost in the darkness; nor was there much likelihood that it would again come within the range of my vision, for I knew that the Vulture planned to lie offshore in about the same position for several hours before he crept stealthily in to the anchorage outside the cove.

I do not know how long I swam, but I had about come to the conclusion that I had missed the island and was headed out to sea when I heard the welcome surge of surf ahead. It seemed incredible that I had come this far without being devoured, but I knew that there was still plenty of time. In fact, the danger might be greater close to shore than farther out; but I tried to put these thoughts from my mind and, now that shore was almost an accomplished fact, develop some plan of action for the immediate future. Nor was I long in coming to a conclusion as to the best procedure to adopt in introducing myself into this domain of the arch enemy of the man whose lieutenant I had been for more than two years.

Presently I saw a light ahead of me, and toward this

welcome beacon I made my way. I am a strong swimmer and endowed with great endurance, so the long swim had taken little toll upon my energy. And it was with powerful, even strokes that I approached the light, which proved, as I had guessed, to be aboard a ship – the pirate ship of the dread Portuguese.

Without hesitation I swam toward the craft, and as I approached it I called out, 'Ship, ahoy!'

Instantly I heard excited voices coming from the deck of the vessel, and then a gruff voice demanded, 'Who are you?' and 'Where away?'

'Lower a rope!' I shouted. 'I want to see the Portuguese.'

Now, a deep, coarse voice boomed over the ship's side. 'I am the Portuguese. Who are you and what do you want? How the hell did you get here?'

'Take me aboard and I'll tell you,' I replied. 'I've got some information for you that you'll be glad to have, but I'm not going to stay here in the ocean all night.'

They lowered a rope, and I clambered to the deck. In the light of a lantern I was inspected by a gang of ruffians quite as vicious in appearance as those I had so recently quit. I recognized the Portuguese immediately, for I had seen him for a few moments on the beach at the time of my landing upon the Vulture's island. He was a coarse, brutal-appearing fellow, not at all like the aristocratic Vulture, and his coarse voice as well as his repellant features reflected his low origin.

'Well,' he growled, 'who are you, and what do you want?'

'My name is Lafitte,' I replied. 'For two years I have been second in command to the Vulture.'

I heard the low intaking of breath that reflected the astonishment which this statement provoked. I saw dirty paws go the hilts of knives and the butts of pistols.

'And you come aboard the Portuguese's ship and admit it?' demanded the chief incredulously.

'I have been trying to escape from the Vulture for a long time,' I replied, 'in fact ever since I heard about the Portuguese I have wanted to join him. This is the first chance I have had.'

The big fellow grunted. 'What have you heard about me?' he demanded.

'That you're the most powerful man in these waters, sort of a sultan, and that a fellow's lucky to be with you.'

He nodded approvingly. 'That's right,' he boasted. Suddenly his lids narrowed. 'You haven't told me how you got here,' he growled. 'You didn't swim all the way from the Vulture's island, and I'm damned sure you didn't walk.'

'I swam from his ship,' I explained. 'It's lying offshore about a mile, waiting to land and attack you – that's what I swam in to tell you. Now, do I join up with you or don't I?'

'If you've told me the truth, you do, but if this is a trick –' He stopped speaking and just stood there glaring at me. The Portuguese had the meanest eyes I ever saw in a human race, or in any other sort of a face. They were bad enough when he just looked natural, but when he glared they suggested to me some particularly foul and obscene death beyond the imagination of man.

'It's no trick,' I assured him. 'The Vulture is coming in without lights and will anchor outside your cove. Then he will land his entire force, with the exception of three men, and attack your place on land. He is looking for a woman you brought out from Singapore; he has given orders to kill all men. You can keep me under guard until you know I have told you the truth.'

For a moment the hulking brute stood in silence. I guessed that thought required almost a physical effort on his part. One could almost see an idea wandering around in the muddy chaos of his brain searching for a way out.

Finally he turned to one standing near him. 'Put him in the brig,' he ordered, 'until we see what happens.'

The brig was a black and filthy hole smelling of bilge water and worse. There I sat on the floor for long hours; there was nothing else to sit on. The air was stuffy, the heat oppressive: I almost suffocated. For a long while the silence was unbroken, and then, faintly, I heard shots. The sound of them increased in volume as the explosion of cartridges multiplied in number, and mingled with them I could hear the cries and shouts of men. After fifteen or twenty minutes they died down and finally ceased, and again came the silence.

For half an hour I sat there waiting, wondering how the battle had gone. If the Vulture had been victorious he would take this ship, and I should have the alternative of remaining where I was and dying of starvation or making my presence known and being disposed of by Ludang; and I imagined that

Ludang would make me pay for that clip to the jaw.

Presently I heard footsteps outside the brig, and a moment later a key turned in the lock and the door was swung open. Outside stood a half-naked cutthroat with a lantern in his hand. He jerked a stubby thumb upward. 'The chief wants you,' he announced.

I followed him on deck and then down a companionway to the Portuguese's cabin, from behind the closed door of which I heard loud voices. My escort pounded on the door with the hilt of his dagger.

'Who's there?' demanded the voice of the Portuguese.

'You sent me for the prisoner,' replied my escort. 'He's here.'

'Send him in!' shouted the chief.

As I entered the smoke-filled room I saw two men and two women. Three of them were sitting about a table on which were bottles and glasses, the fourth, one of the women, was half sitting, half reclining on a bunk at the far side of the cabin. The room was poorly lighted by a single oil lamp, and the woman's face was in the shadow of an upper bunk, so that I could not have seen her features clearly had I been interested in trying to do so, which I was not.

The other woman was white and of the type one might have expected to see in such surroundings. Her face was hard and marked by dissipation. If she had ever been pretty the last vestiges of it had faded long ago. She was a coarse, fat slattern with a mop of peroxide-yellow hair.

As I stepped into the room their conversation ceased and they sat appraising me for a moment. From the depth of the bunk at the far side of the room came a startled exclamation, quickly smothered. The woman at the table turned in the direction of the bunk. 'What's the matter with the Queen of Diamonds?' she demanded.

'Can't a girl sneeze!' came the quick reply.

'Sure, dearie, but I thought you was chokin'. Get up an' look at the new one; he ain't hard to look at, dearie.'

'I see him,' replied the other girl. But she couldn't see me, for when I glanced in her direction I saw that she had moved so that her face was hidden by the bulging form of the other woman, a discovery which did not interest me and made scarcely any impression on me.

'Well,' said the Portuguese in what was evidently intended for a jovial tone, 'you did me a good turn and you didn't trick me: now what do you want?'

'I want to join you,' I replied, 'as a mate.'

'And then betray me as you did the Vulture,' snapped the Portuguese, suddenly ferocious again.

'I owed the Vulture nothing,' I replied. 'I did not join him of my own free will; I was a prisoner. I came to you differently.'

'That's right,' said the fat woman at the table.

'Shut up, Lil,' growled the second man. 'Don't show so much interest in this new one or I'll slit you open and toss you to the sharks.'

The woman arose from her chair and leaning on the table, her arms akimbo, broke into such a tirade of profane and obscene abuse as I had never heard before, while the man reached for his knife. What the outcome would have been had no one interfered I do not know, but the Portuguese did interfere. Seizing a champagne bottle he pounded vigorously on the table, demanding silence, and the two brutes obeyed him.

'Pedro,' he said, addressing the man, 'you two fight too much. I am tired of it. I get fighting enough on deck; down here I want peace. One of these days I'll knife you both, do you understand?'

Pedro nodded. 'I understand, Chief,' he replied in a surly tone.

'Why aren't you like the Queen of Diamonds and me?' continued the Portuguese. 'We never fight; be loving like we are.' He looked over toward the woman in the bunk. 'Come here, Queen!' he cried, 'and show them how we love.'

There was a moment's silence, during which the woman made no move to obey. 'Not now, please,' she said. 'I do not feel like it; I am ill.'

I was struck by a haunting familiarity in the quality of the voice; it reminded me of someone but of whom I could not recall, and an instant later I had forgotten it as I listened to the Portuguese recount the engagement in which his forces had run off those of the Vulture.

'We had every man on deck with plenty of firearms and ammunition, and we kept a sharp lookout for the boats from the *Señorita.*' The Portuguese rubbed his great palms together in appreciation. 'We kept well hidden and very quiet. After a while we heard an oarlock squeak. Next we saw a shadow on the water, and then another shadow and another. It was then that I gave the command to fire.

'They didn't stand it for very long, by God, no! They commenced to turn and pull back out to sea, but we got a lot of them. I hope we did not kill the Vulture. I want to see him die. I want to kill him with my own hands.'

The Portuguese asked me to drink; he poured a tumbler full of champagne and handed it to me, and I took a courtesy swallow and set the tumbler down.

'You do not like my wine?' he demanded. 'You do not like to drink with me?' Again his tone was ugly. It was evident that he was an ugly character and a bully.

'I am not like you,' I said. 'I cannot do two things well. I cannot drink below and fight on deck. My business is fighting, not drinking. Had I been a heavy drinker I could not have swum in from the Vulture's ship to warn you. Do you want a fighting man or a drinking man as mate?'

'By God! you are right,' he cried. 'There are many times that we need a sober head on board.'

Presently he let me go, sending Pedro to show me where I was to bunk, a stuffy little cabin near the galley; but at least I was to occupy it alone. Before I went to sleep I recalled all that had passed during this eventful night. I compared the Portuguese and the Vulture and decided that of the two I would rather serve the latter; at least he had once been a gentleman. Even their tastes in women marked the difference in their cultural stations in life. Of course I hadn't seen the other woman in the Portuguese's cabin: but I had seen Lil, and I assumed that the woman on the bunk was of the same sort. I recalled the strange familiarity of her voice and then I fell to thinking of *La Diablesa.* The thought that she had turned against me and betrayed me to the Vulture rankled in my breast to such an extent that I was brought up suddenly by the suggestion it implied, that I really loved *La Diablesa.* Then I thought of Daisy Juke, and that helped to put the other idea from my mind.

I was thinking of her sweet loveliness and her purity as I fell asleep, but this vision of hers was distorted just a little by the memory of that last meeting when I had smelled liquor on her breath.

I was up early the next morning, donning my shorts, my sole wordly possession; and was soon on deck. As I stepped out into the morning air I saw a woman standing at the rail looking out to sea. She was not Lil – I could tell that by her slender, graceful figure – so she must be the other woman whose face I had not seen.

I was only a few feet behind her as I emerged from the companionway, and she must have heard me, for she turned otward me instantly as though she had been surprised in some overt act. As I saw her face I gasped.

'Daisy!' I cried. 'Daisy Juke!'

Her lower lip trembled as she whispered my name; and then she said, 'I didn't want you to see me.'

'What are you doing here?' I demanded.

'You saw,' she replied.

'But you must be a prisoner – you – ' A thought sprang to my mind; but no, it was preposterous. 'You were not in the cabin last night, there were only two women there: Lil and the Queen of Diamonds.' The latter, I knew, was the notorious demimondaine of the brothels of Singapore.

She looked up at me, a sudden defiance in her eyes. 'I am the Queen of Diamonds,' she said.

I was stunned; I couldn't believe it. I sought some explanation that might excuse her. 'But you are the Portuguese's prisoner,' I urged. 'He stole you and brought you with him against your will.'

She shook her head. 'I came willingly. What difference did it make?' she cried bitterly. 'He is as good as any of them, and he brought me farther away from – from Glenora – from home. I want to get far away. I want to get where no one will see me. And now you, of all others, have to be the first person I meet.' She looked at me accusingly. 'Why did you have to come on deck now?' she cried almost fiercely. 'In another moment you would never have been able to know.'

'What do you mean?' I asked.

She pointed over the rail. 'Look,' she said.

I stepped to her side and looked down into the clear waters of the cove. Just below the surface a great shark glided into the shadows beneath the ship's keel.

For a while we stood there in silence, then I laid my hand on hers. 'How did it happen?' I asked. 'What brought you to – to this?'

'The blood of old Max Juke,' she replied bitterly.

'But what about Frank? You and he were to have been married.'

'I got to drinking,' she said dully. 'I couldn't stop. I was drunk the night Mrs Adams gave a big dinner to announce the engagement; it was never announced.' She looked up at me suddenly. 'Perhaps it was just as well. I never loved Frank Adams; I loved someone else.'

I must have looked my astonishment. 'Why Daisy, you never went with anyone else. There couldn't have been anyone else.'

'There was – always; but he never spoke to me of love, though sometimes I was sure he loved me.'

'I can't imagine whom it could have been.'

'No, *you* couldn't,' she said wearily. 'What difference does it make now who knows? I might as well tell you. It was you, Johnny.'

I was so surprised that I couldn't say a word, but somehow there was no answering thrill with the knowledge of the thing I had longed for all my life. I must have realized that this wasn't the Daisy Juke I had loved.

'Don't try to say anything, Johnny,' she begged. 'There isn't anything for you to say. I'm going to tell you the rest. It hurts to tell the man I love, Johnny, but I'm going to do it.'

'You needn't, Daisy. I don't want to hear it.'

'But I'm going to tell you. After the break between Frank and me I got to running around with a bootlegger. He introduced me to a Chinese who smuggled opium. I ran away with the damn Chink. He brought me to Singapore, and there I got tired of him and threw him over. Then I went on the town.'

She spoke the last sentence all in a single breath, as though she wanted to get it over with as quickly as possible.

'Poor child!' That was all I could say.

She shook her head. 'It's the blood, the curse of blood. It made you a pirate; it made me a – what I am.' She turned to go away. 'Goodbye, Johnny.'

'Where are you going?'

'Below.'

'Then why goodbye? I'll see you again. We'll get out of this and start over again somewhere.'

She shook her head. 'I wonder if we can. I wonder if we can ever escape our putrid blood streams, either here or hereafter. Start over again somewhere.' She was walking toward the companionway. 'Yes, start over again somewhere,' she repeated as she descended toward the cabin of the Portuguese.

I turned back to the rail and stood staring down at the great shark. I thought of Daisy Juke and of *La Diablesa*, of the Vulture and the Portuguese and myself. I wondered if we were any more accountable to God for our acts on earth than the shark.

From below came the muffled report of a revolver shot. Beneath my breath I cursed the memory of Max Juke.

Chapter Thirteen

TO THE VICTOR

THE PORTUGUESE WANTED to throw Daisy's body overboard to the sharks, but I persuaded him to let me take it ashore and give it as decent a burial as conditions permitted. He thought I was a fool and said so, but he let me have some men to help me and a blanket to wrap her in.

It was a pathetic burial, but only I knew how pathetic. I am not a soft man, but the tears came to my eyes as we laid that pitiful little form in its shallow grave and covered it forever from the sight of man.

As we pulled back to the schooner I was thinking of the sorry tricks that life had played on me. If, years ago, I had known that Daisy loved me how different everything might have been for both of us. We might have gone happily on together, loving, loved, and respected, environment saving us from the curse of heredity. Yet I wondered. Perhaps the Juke and the Lafitte that coursed through our veins would have dragged us down sooner or later.

I thought of the only two loves my life had known: the one that had come to this that I had just buried and the other that had betrayed me while our arms were about one another in love. My thoughts were bitter thoughts, arousing in my breast a longing for revenge.

I determined to kill the Portuguese. He had possessed the woman I had loved, the woman who had loved me. I would kill him, but not until he had served my purpose in consummating another vengeance. That would be on *La Diablesa.* It would have to be indirect. I couldn't bring myself to kill her, of course; but I could strike at her through another – I could kill the Vulture. If he were dead, she would have no protector.

For a long time I had wished to kill him – for several reasons. One was jealousy. Perhaps that was the strongest. Another was greed. Yes, I have an aggregation of lovely characteristics. I coveted his ship and the leadership of his band of cutthroats. The genes of old Jean Lafitte, the French Corsair of the Gulf of Mexico, were running true to form.

And to achieve my gentle destiny, if it were destiny, I needed the Portuguese. Therefore I must, for the time, forego the pleasure of killing him. It never once occurred to me that I might fail in these ventures and be killed myself. Great accomplishments are not fostered by doubts.

Large in my mind loomed the memory of *La Diablesa.* It dwarfed that of Daisy Juke. I wanted to see her again. I wanted to reproach her for her treachery. I wanted to witness her rage and consternation when I killed the Vulture.

How she had fooled me! Making me think that she hated him, accepting my love, and then striking me down at his feet to be killed. How I would revel in my vengeance! But would I? Try to hate her as I would, I still knew that I loved her. Yet my determination did not waver. No matter what the cost, I would carry out my plan.

When I boarded the schooner, I sought the Portuguese. He was in a terrible humor. The suicide of the Queen of Diamonds had robbed him of a plaything. His sorrow was not that of the lover. There was nothing fine or decent about it. It was the rage of a beast that had been deprived of something it desired and with no one directly responsible upon whom it could vent its spleen and take its revenge.

I entered his cabin, therefore, at a bad moment. He was

drinking brandy with Pedro and his second mate, a huge Negro called Nigger Joe. The three eyed me venomously. Almost immediately the Portuguese started accusing me of being responsible for his woman's death. He said that after I had gone ashore to bury her, Nigger Joe had told him that he had seen me arguing with her on deck just a few minutes before she went below and shot herself.

'Don't be a fool,' I told him. 'What could I have said to her that might have made her kill herself? As a matter of fact I kept her from killing herself when I came on deck. She was about to throw herself overboard to the sharks.'

The Portuguese spat on the floor. 'You expect me to believe that?' he demanded. 'You done something to her. She wasn't the same after you come into the cabin last night. Lil noticed it. She was a changed woman. I don't know what I ever let you live for, but you ain't goin' to live no longer.' He drew his pistol. I was unarmed. It looked like the end, but I just stood there and laughed at him – a dirty sneering kind of laugh. It got his goat. 'What are you laughin' at?' he bellowed.

'You. . . .'

That made him pretty mad. He was shaking, he was so angry. 'So you're laughin' at me! And what's so damned funny about me?'

'You haven't any sense. If you had, you wouldn't be sittin' down here with a couple of nitwits swilling brandy while the Vulture, probably shorthanded from last night's battle, is heading for his home port just a few hours ahead of you. Why don't you get busy and get after him instead of threatening to kill the only intelligent man you got aboard?'

The big brute just sat there and stared at me. He didn't seem to be able to comprehend that anyone had dared speak to him as I had. I saw that I had gained a little advantage. Like most of his kind, the fellow was a coward. His blatant, bullying manner was the defense mechanism with which he sought to hide it. It seemed within the range of possibilities that I might outbluff him. I tried it.

'Put down that gun,' I said, 'and listen to me.' He lowered the muzzle of his weapon until it rested on the table. 'I've got it in for the Vulture,' I continued. 'He stole my girl and then tried to kill me. If you weren't a lot of drunken, yellow bums I could show you how you could take his island and his ship.

He's got enough swag on that island to buy half of Lisbon, and you sit here and guzzle brandy because you haven't the brains or the guts to go and take it. You make me sick – the whole dirty bunch of you.'

Pedro leaped from his chair and came for me, a wicked-looking knife in his hand. 'I'm a dirty bum, am I? I ain't got no guts, ain't I?'

We're taught jujitsu by experts on the police forces of California. That training had saved my life before. It saved it then. I caught the wrist of his knife hand, swung quickly around, and threw him over my head. I threw him hard, too. He lit in a crumpled heap against the wall of the cabin, his knife falling to the floor. I picked it up and tossed it onto the table in front of the Portuguese.

'You've got a new first mate,' I told him. 'That is you have if you've got any brains at all. What do you say? We can put out after the Vulture with the tide.'

The Portuguese rose and stepped over to the unconscious form of Pedro. Stooping, he removed the fellow's two pistols; then he straightened up and handed them to me.

'You're goin' to need 'em,' he said, 'if you're goin' to be first mate of this craft long. You'd better take the knife, too.'

'When do we sail?'

'With the tide.'

Well, we sailed. That was some trip. The men didn't take to me. God! but they were a hard lot – foulest scum of the foulest waterfronts. Many of them were absolutely fearless, but they'd rather stab a man in the back than the front any time – it must have been just the ethics of their profession. They resented the fact that I was a stranger, that I kept myself clean, and that I insisted that the ship be kept clean. When I had come aboard it had been the filthiest thing I'd ever seen afloat. It had been so filled with various assorted stinks that one could almost have carved them with a knife. Bilge water and garlic predominated. I cleaned it up. But I had to kill one man and cripple two others in the process. After that my popularity increased. . . .

The Portuguese, having at least a rudimentary sense of humor, had put Pedro, now a common sailor, in Nigger Joe's watch. I didn't appreciate the Machiavellian touch in this assignment until I learned from a member of the crew that

Pedro and Nigger Joe were mortal enemies, the former having taken advantage of his position as first mate to delegate all the onerous and unpleasant duties to his inferior; then they had both aspired to Lil. She had belonged to Nigger Joe first, but Pedro had taken her away. Notwithstanding the fact that neither now commanded her charms – the Portuguese having appropriated her – their hatred for one another still persisted.

It is noticeable how prevalent are hatreds among people of the moral and mental types to which these men belonged. What passes for friendship among them is based solely upon mercenary considerations. They mistook lust for love. Hatred is the only genuine sentiment they may boast. Perhaps a careful analysis would reveal for the remainder of mankind a similar picture painted in less vivid colors upon a background of hypocrisy and moral cowardice.

Yes I was in nice company – sweet little playmates, indeed, were these, my fellow pirates. But was I any better? Honest self-analysis is fatal. The test of true friendship is the secret sacrifice that one would make for a friend, where no reciprocation nor any applause were possible. If you think you really love a woman, ask yourself if you would respect and admire her and wish to spend the rest of your life with her if she were a man, forsaking all others. And hatred? I was full of it. I hated them all: the Portuguese, Pedro, Nigger Joe, Ludang, the Vulture, *La Diablesa*. Yes, I hated even *La Diablesa*. But then, of course, she had wronged me foully – far more than any of the others had wronged me.

These pleasant thoughts were running through my mind one night as I stood on deck while the ship, rising and falling to long swells, cut silently through the black sea beneath an overcast sky, her course set for the Vulture's nameless island.

I was in the shadow of the deckhouse. I could see Pedro forward, his squat bulk dimly outlined in the faint light of a ship's lantern. He was leaning over the rail, staring idly down upon the black swells, rising, falling. They hold a fascination, especially at night; it is almost hypnotic in its effects. Perhaps that is why Pedro did not hear the approach of a man behind him.

It was Nigger Joe. From the manner in which he was sneaking up behind his arch enemy I surmised that his designs were evil – perhaps lethal. I indulged in a mental shrug. What interest had I in the welfare of either of those cutthroats? If one killed the other, the world would be better off by that much, and it made little difference to the world or me which one were killed.

I saw that Nigger Joe had his knife out. He was going to stab Pedro in the back. Now there are some acts that are peculiarly repulsive. Stabbing a man in the back is one of these. It irritates me immeasurably. Even though the man to be stabbed were the utterest scum and deserved death, I felt that I should do something about it.

Almost simultaneously with this Christian urge three things happened very suddenly. Pedro must have heard or felt the presence of the man behind him, for he wheeled suddenly. Nigger Joe's knife flashed upward. I fired....

With a howl of pain and rage the black leaped back, his knife clattering to the deck. Grasping his shattered right hand in his left, Nigger Joe turned and fled. Pedro took a shot at him and missed; then he turned toward me. He couldn't see who I was until I came within the radius of the dim light. When he recognized me he was far more surprised than he had been when he had seen Nigger Joe about to attempt his life. He just stood there staring at me in a dumb sort of way.

I heard men running. Two shots in the dead of night aboard a craft like ours might mean almost anything. The Portuguese barged into view. Pedro was still staring at me uncomprehendingly. 'That was a fine shot,' he said. Then the Portuguese confronted us.

'What's goin' on?' he demanded.

Pedro told him.

'Oh,' said the Portuguese, 'is that all?' He seemed much relieved. Like prosperity in civilization, mutiny on a craft such as ours is always just around the corner. 'Where's Nigger Joe? Did you kill him?'

'No; I didn't try to.'

'Where'd you get him?'

'In the right hand. I don't know how bad.'

'It was a fine shot,' said Pedro.

'He won't be no good now for a long time,' mused the Portuguese.

'He never was,' I said. 'Pedro should be second mate.'

So Pedro became second mate of the *Coruña*. His emotions

must have been mixed. He had lost his job at first mate because of me, and I had supplanted him. Now I had saved his life and had him appointed second mate. But I didn't expect any gratitude. My sole reason for wanting him as second mate was that I could watch him better.

In due time we raised the Vulture's island, and after dark we sneaked around to windward of it. The harbor is on the lee side of the island during the prevailing winds. No one ever goes to the opposite coast. It is rocky and barren. Cliffs run right to the sea. There is no beach nor any landing place, or at least there was not supposed to be. But I had found one. It was after I had succeeded in getting the Vulture to try out my pirate breeding plan. We had extended the clearing and put in more crops. During this work I had discovered what appeared to be the remains of a very old trail. Although it was overgrown it was still plain. It led away from the clearing toward the opposite side of the island. It aroused my curiosity, so I followed it. I suppose that was the police instinct in me.

It cut through a short distance of jungle and then out into the barren lands. Even there it was plain, though, and I followed it to the coast. It led me to the summit of the cliffs above a tiny cove, and when I looked over I saw that a trail had been cut down to a narrow strip of beach. I hadn't gone down; my curisoity had been satisfied. I hadn't the slightest idea that I should ever make any use of my knowledge of this backdoor entrance to the Vulture's stronghold, but I didn't tell him nor anyone else of my discovery. I was sure that he knew nothing of it.

We stood off the windward coast until dawn; then we crept in carefully, looking for the cove. It wasn't easy to find, but at last I located it. We dropped anchor and lowered the boats.

The Portuguese left a few men, whom he thought he could trust, to guard the *Coruña*. The rest of us, about fifty strong, pulled for the cove. We were a sweet company. Most of us were naked above the waist. To protect our heads from the tropic sun we wore colored handkerchiefs. Many had brilliant sashes wound around their middles. The majority sported earrings, and there were several with noserings.

The Portuguese had issued a big tumbler of rum to each of the crew before we left the ship, and had further aroused them by tales of the rich loot we'd divide.

From the top of the cliff I led the way along the trail toward the Vulture's nest. The Portuguese had delegated the command to me because I knew the lay of the land, and the men had instructions to take their orders from me. Single file we wound through the strip of jungle that separated the barren land from the clearing. At the trail's end I raised my hand as a signal for those behind me to halt, and the signal was passed on down the line.

Before me I could see a number of men and women working among the crops. They were virtually slaves. And while they owed their slavery to me, they also owed me their lives. Had it not been for me the Vulture would have killed them – at least the men. The women would have been killed eventually. I had never treated them harshly, and I knew that while they could have no love for me they trusted me more and hated me less than any other of their captors.

Telling the Portuguese, who was directly behind me, to keep the men quiet, I stepped out into the clearing. Those nearest me recognized me instantly, and I saw surprise reflected in their expressions. I moved toward them and called them together, so that presently they were gathered around me. I asked them if the Vulture had returned, and they said he had. The thing that had surprised them was that I had come from the jungle. They thought that I was still with the Vulture, and couldn't understand how I had gotten past them and into the jungle without their having seen me.

I explained that the Vulture had tried to kill me but that I had escaped and returned with a force of men large enough to capture the island. I told them that if they would join me we could take the place easily and that I would see that they were treated right in return for their support. What I really wished of them was that they wouldn't take sides against us; for as far as their active assistance was concerned they wouldn't be of much value to me, as they were not armed and very few of them impressed me as being fighting men.

They were so sore at the Vulture that they quickly promised to do anything I asked of them; so now, assured that no alarm would be raised by these people, I summoned the remainder of my choice aggregation from the jungle and started off toward the compound and the men's quarters, neither of which was visible from this field.

I had carefully explained the lay of the land to both the Portuguese and Pedro. When we reached a point beyond which we could not hope to advance without detection, I gave the prearranged signal and we all started at a run for our objectives. The Portuguese, with the majority of the men, went for the barracks. I led a half-dozen men, among whom was Pedro, toward the compound, where I expected to find the Vulture. When we arrived, no one was in sight, and I instructed my followers to search the rooms, capturing the Vulture alive, if possible. They also had orders to harm no women or the Chinese cook, Kao.

I went directly to the Vulture's room. He was not there. Then I ran down the veranda to *La Diablesa*'s quarters. Somehow my heart beat very fast at the prospect of seeing her again, but I kept telling myself that I hated her.

I entered unceremoniously and found her seated at her dressing table. She turned, and when she recognized me she stood up and faced me. Her face went very white, and she swayed a little as though she were about to fall. 'John!' she cried. 'He told me that you were dead.'

'It's not your fault that I'm not, you damned snake. I ought to kill you.'

Her eyes went wide, and then she drew herself up very straight. 'Get out of here!' she said.

'Where is the Vulture?'

She shook her head. 'Get out of here!'

'I'll see to you after I've attended to him. Stay in your room. I have fifty men here with me. They'd as lief slit your throat as not.' Then I turned and went out on the veranda and started back toward the Vulture's room. As I passed a doorway I was struck a heavy blow on the side of the head. It didn't knock me out completely, just dazed me for a few seconds, but in that time I was disarmed. I recall that I could hear the shouts and cries and curses of men, mingled with the reports of firearms and knew that the fight was on at the barracks. Then I felt a gun poked into my ribs and heard the cold voice of the Vulture in my ear. 'Come with me to *La Diablesa*'s room, my dear friend. We have three matters to discuss.'

'It will be a pleasure.'

'It will be a very great pleasure – for me,' he assured me.

Some of my men appeared on the veranda. He told them

that if they came nearer he would kill me, and then he whispered to me to send them away. If I didn't, he would shoot me where I stood. I knew that he would, and so I told them to go to the barracks and get into the fight there.

He pushed me ahead of him into the presence of *La Diablesa*. 'I have brought your lover to you,' he said in a nasty tone. She said nothing. 'I could not have hoped for anything so good as this. I am going to cut out his heart right here in front of you, the ——.' He applied to me the vilest epithet that he could lay his tongue to. First he stole you. Then he deserted to the Portuguese and betrayed my plans. Now he comes to kill me. The Vulture does not die so easily. But your lover shall die, and his men shall all be killed. You can hear my brave lads killing them now. I want him to know that he has failed – failed in everything. Watch now, *La Diablesa*.'

He stepped behind me and secured my wrists; then he turned me around so that my left side was toward *La Diablesa*. 'So that you can see better, my dear,' he said. He drew his knife. 'You shall see the heart that has beaten in rhythm to your love, *La Diablesa*.' He raised his blade. Death seemed very near, but that did not seem to concern me so much as the fact that these two would gloat over my failure. I deliberately kept my eyes averted from *La Diablesa*. I wanted to look at her, but I would not.

It seemed to me that the Vulture took a very long time in carrying out his design. Perhaps he hoped to force some sign of fear from me that would add to his enjoyment of the situation, but I gave none. I just stood there, waiting. I was really surprised myself that I should be so unconcerned about death. It was not through courage. It was more because of a realization that for long I had expected a violent death and the knowledge that my life was worthless – that no one would mourn me and that the world would be better off without me.

There was a sharp report, and the Vulture lunged forward upon me almost throwing me to the floor; then he slumped in a shrunken heap at my feet. I looked at *La Diablesa*. She stood there wide-eyed, a smoking revolver clutched in her right hand. She was very white, and she swayed upon her feet. I thought she was going to fall, so I stepped forward to support her, forgetting that my hands were bound behind me. At that, she wheeled and leveled the revolver at me.

'Get out of here!' she ordered. 'I was going to kill you, too; but I can't. Get out!'

'I'll be rather helpless out there with my hands tied behind me.'

She picked up the Vulture's knife and came and cut my bonds. When I stepped into the compound I realized that the fight was still on at the barracks. I could hear the shots and the raucous cries of the combatants. My place was there; so I hurried out into the compound in time to see the remnants of the Vulture's company backing away, exchanging shots with some of the Portuguese's men who were pressing forward. Ludang was among the former. As he came through the gateway, he turned to run for one of the rooms, possibly to search for the Vulture. As he turned, he saw me. He paused in surprise; then all his pent hatred of me was reflected in his snarling face as he raised his revolver to shoot me down. I beat him to it, and he dropped in his tracks, clutching at his breast.

We finished the other men in short order. The fight was over. We had taken the stronghold of the Vulture! The Portuguese was mad with elation. He ordered us to kill every man on the island. I called his attention to the fact that I had promised protection to the prisoners.

'I'm giving orders here,' he bellowed.

'Then you'd better give orders to leave those men alone – and the women, too. I'll shoot any man that lays a hand on one of them.'

I turned my back on them then and went to look for Kao. I wanted to be sure they didn't kill him. He was my best friend there; and, besides, he was a good cook.

It's difficult to understand how yellow bullies like the Portuguese are. Even with my back turned toward him he was afraid to shoot me, as I had guessed he would be.

I found Kao hiding in his room behind the kitchen. To say he was relieved when he saw me would be putting it far too mildly. He almost wept for joy and relief. I asked him to get me something to eat, and I sat on a corner of the kitchen table and talked with him while he was preparing it.

'You see *La Diablesa* yet?' he asked. 'I betee you she glad see you.'

'I saw her, and I hope to God it's the last time.'

'Walla you meany?' demanded Kao.

I told him how she had double-crossed me and nearly gotten me killed by the Vulture just before we sailed for Singapore.

'You damn fool,' said Kao. 'She save your life.' Then he told me that which filled me with shame and remorse.

La Diablesa had seen the Vulture approaching and had known that it would be impossible for us to break away before he saw us. She knew him better than any other – knew his insane jealousy. If he had suspected that she was willingly accepting my caresses he would have killed us both. That I might seek to win her was no offense in the eyes of the Vulture – provided I did not succeed. If *La Diablesa* repulsed me, why that was a feather in the Vulture's cap – it puffed his ego. She had thought and acted very quickly, and she had saved our lives.

I determined to see her at once and ask her forgiveness for the brutal words I had spoken, and with this intention in mind I hurried to her quarters. Before I reached them I heard her voice raised in protest, and when I burst into the room I saw Pedro and the Portuguese there. Pedro was sitting astride a chair, laughing. The Portuguese was holding *La Diablesa* with his great, dirty paws and trying to drag her lips to his. I crossed the room in two strides, seized the Portuguese by his long, greasy hair and dragged him away. Then I wheeled him about and struck him a blow in the face that sent him reeling into a corner.

Without paying any more attention to the two men, I took *La Diablesa*'s hand. She tried to draw away, but I held her. 'You must listen to me, *La Diablesa*. I have come to apologize. I didn't know the truth until Kao just told me. I really thought that you had double-crossed me.'

'That is why I hate you – that you could believe such a thing of me.'

'Please forgive me. My only excuse is that I loved you so much I was crazy with jealousy.'

Her eyes suddenly went wide in fright as she looked across my shoulder. Then she screamed, and merged with her scream was the sharp staccato of a shot.

As I wheeled and drew, I swung *La Diablesa* behind me, but there was no need for any precaution. The Portuguese lay sprawled face down on the floor. Pedro still sat in his chair, his revolver in his hand.

'He was goin' to shoot you, Chief. I been goin' to kill the bastard for a long time. Now we got a damn good chief – not a yellow coward. The other men, they all be glad.'

'You go tell 'em, Pedro.' I was mighty glad then that I had saved Pedro's life that time.

As he left the room I turned back to *La Diablesa*. 'I've got the island, the loot, and two ships,' I said. 'All else I need in the world is you. Will you come back to me?'

She came and put her arms around my neck. 'I have never been away, Johnny. I tried to be, but I couldn't.'

That was two years ago. *La Diablesa* and I live in Paris now – quiet and respectable married folk – but we are not known as *La Diablesa* and John Lafitte. Only our cook, Kao, knows; and he would die before he would tell.

If Pedro hasn't had his throat slit, he is doubtless the scourge of the South Seas, with his two ships, his nameless island, and his sweet company of cutthroats.